Bernard McKenna and Colin Bostock-Smith

Encyclopocalypse Publications
www.encyclopocalypse.com

Contents

One

Fiona Harris had been married to Arthur Harris for ten years to the day when she left him.

It took Arthur by surprise. He'd left his office early that day and spent an embarrassing and expensive ten minutes in a City florists, buying a stunted Japanese "bonsai" tree. It was, in his opinion, an ugly little perversion of nature, and hideously overpriced, too, but Fiona would love it. Using both hands to carry the thing, in its delicate gift-wrapping, he made a hazardous journey along the crowded City pavements until he reached a taxi-queue. There he enjoyed an unequalled opportunity to witness the human race at its worst, as one by one other travellers noted how encumbered he was with the tree, and took the opportunity to cheat him out of his turn for a taxi. To secure a ride for himself and his Japanese-type tree, it took a Japanese-type kamikaze leap into the road. Fortunately the taxi stopped just in time, Arthur argued his way into the back seat and eventually the thing took him and his tree home. Arthur didn't object to all this trouble. It was, he felt, the kind of thing that any normal happily married man suffered gladly.

Home was a flat, several floors up an anonymous-looking block that boasted a view over Regent's Park. Arthur had hoped to make the lift without meeting anyone. It was embarrassing to be seen clutching a gift-wrapped tree. It spoke too loudly of a personal intimate scene to come. Like meeting a snooty neighbour in the supermarket just as you buy a bargain offer in loo-paper. So head down, moving fast, Arthur slid through the front door, and slid straight into the awful caretaker.

"Ah, Mr. Harris! I've got some good news for you," said the caretaker.

"Oh."

For a moment Arthur wondered if the man had found a new job. No, the news couldn't be that good.

Arthur walked on to the lift doors. Waiting there were an elderly Darby-and-Joan couple he knew slightly. Mr. and Mrs. Kemp. They nodded politely. The awful caretaker shuffled after him, and gallantly pressed the lift button with a long knobbly finger.

"Oh, yes," he went on. "You'll be very pleased to know that you're not the only one who has stuff stolen."

"Oh, that *is* good news." Arthur wondered why he bothered. Irony was lost on the caretaker.

"Oh, yes—eggs, yoghurt, sliced bread, potatoes—*front* doors."

"Somebody is stealing front doors?"

"No no no." The caretaker was patient in the face of Arthur's stupidity. "That's where it's all going from. Outside the front doors. I blame the Italians."

"What?"

"The Italians in number twenty-three." The pure light of xenophobia gleamed in the awful caretaker's eye. "Because of the war, you know."

"And stealing my milk is some sort of revenge?" asked Arthur.

"That's right."

The lift came. Arthur and Mr. and Mrs. Kemp got in, and the doors closed on the caretaker's skinny face. They began the journey upwards.

"It's about time we got rid of him," Arthur told

the couple. "Last week he blamed the Japanese, in fifty-six. Next week it'll be the Germans on my floor."

They smiled but said nothing. Arthur got out at his floor. He wondered if they too believed in the Italians' fanatical fascist vengeance. He hoicked his keys out of his pocket, unlocked his door, and went in, closing the door sharply behind him to announce his arrival.

The noise brought Fiona out of the bedroom, into the entrance hall. She looked at Arthur as if she had never seen him before in her life.

Arthur in his turn looked at her with unusual fondness. Ten years and she hadn't changed a bit. Well, perhaps just a bit. Perhaps the chin, which was always a little firm, now jutted with even greater determination. And the eyes had exchanged the happy naivety they once had for an older, shrewder look. But she was still a striking, attractive woman. *His* striking attractive woman. He was glad to be home.

"Arthur!" Fiona almost snapped. "What are you doing here?"

"I live here!"

"But... you're home early."

Arthur gave her his biggest smile. "Happy anniversary, darling," he said warmly, and offered her the tree.

Fiona did nothing. She didn't take the tree. She didn't say a word. She just looked at Arthur.

Arthur had a moment of doubt. "It *is* today, isn't it?"

"Yes."

"If it's the wrong sort I can change it."

She shook her head.

"Let's have a drink, then," and he made to go into the sitting room.

Fiona's voice rose two tones: "Don't go in there!"

"What...?" And then Arthur twigged. "I get it," he told Fiona with delight. "You've prepared a little surprise for me, and I've come home and spoilt it."

For the first time, Fiona managed a smile. "Yes," she said. Arthur melted inside. How sweet of her to plan a surprise for him.

"That's it," Fiona went on quickly. "So why don't you pop to the pub for an hour, and when you come back I'll be..."

"Right!" That was an even better idea. "I'll just change first."

Still carrying the tree, Arthur strode into the bedroom, and nearly fell over a suitcase.

The bedroom was littered with bags. Holdalls, cases, grips, all chock-a-block with clothes. A half-empty case lay on the bed. Fiona's wardrobe stood open and practically bare. Arthur looked around the room. For a moment he genuinely didn't know what it all meant. Fiona came in behind him and stood by his side, silently.

"What... what's all this?" Arthur managed.

"I'm leaving you."

"When are you coming back?"

"I'm not. I'm going for good."

Good? Arthur thought. What does she mean, Good? Good for what? Good for who?

"What for?" he demanded.

Fiona spoke as if she was lecturing a naughty dog. "We're just not getting on."

"Not getting on?" Arthur couldn't believe it. "We happen to be very happily married!"

"We're not."

"I am."

"I'm not."

"I see," said Arthur, knowing grimly that already he was grasping at straws. "So—it's not a case of we're not happily married. It's you. *Why* not?"

"We always seem to be arguing."

"Rubbish."

"We're arguing now."

This kind of logic is always so infuriating. "No, we are not!" Arthur told her forcibly. "We're… discussing."

"We're arguing."

"You won't get me into an argument by insisting that we're arguing," said Arthur. A neat thrust, he told himself.

"If we're not arguing," Fiona replied, "why are you shouting?"

Arthur began to say, "I am not shouting," and then realized he was. So, deliberately quietly, he began again. "I'm not shouting. I'm not arguing. I'm listening."

"I'm leaving."

She said this with such sickening finality that Arthur lost his cool and began striding about the bedroom.

"Now… now… just… calm… down… right?" he said excitedly. "Just… keep… calm."

"I am," said Fiona. And she was. Arthur stopped his pacing.

"Good. Right. Let's sit down and discuss this rationally," he said, and sat down abruptly on the bed.

Fiona spoiled that move by saying, "No."

"All right." He got to his feet again. "Let's *stand* and discuss it rationally." Then he had a better idea. "I'll get us a drink. And I'll get rid of this bloody tree."

He swept out of the bedroom, through into the sitting room, and had dumped the tree and was starting to pour drinks before he realized that, sitting on the sofa and leafing through *Woman's Journal,* was a black man.

"Evening," said the black man.

So this was it. This was the explanation, sitting right here on his sofa. This was what she needed, was it? Not Arthur. Not smooth civilized Western man. But this—the call of the wild, the passionate primitive, the noble savage. Maybe they really did have bigger... no, Arthur's liberal leanings quashed the thought. He stared at the man. He was black all right, but he was hardly the thick-lipped brutal savage. Rather thin lips, actually. The man looked back politely, waiting for his greeting to be acknowledged. He seemed totally unconcerned. The brazen nerve of it—sitting there, in his house, on his settee....

"Do you realize who I am?" Arthur demanded.

"Er... no...." The man seemed confused.

"I am Arthur Harris." Why did his name always sound so silly when he said it out loud?

"Oh," said the black man.

"Fiona's husband."

"Ah."

The bloody man just didn't seem to care. Of all the bloody nerve...

"You've got a bloody nerve," Arthur told him.

"Sorry...?"

"I'm sure you are, not that I'm here."

"Er..."

"Just how long has this been going on?" Arthur knew he sounded like Lord Chatterley. He didn't care. He over-rode the man's attempt to reply.

"No, don't tell me. Let me guess. Ha! It was last May, when I initiated the new variable accumulation fund, wasn't it! I worked fifteen hours a day on that.

Fifteen! And all that time you were...."

But it was no good going on like this. Mere words were so much chaff. Mechanical responses. Pathetic mouthings. Arthur needed action. Red-blooded, true-blue, hard-hitting action. He clenched his fists and raised his arms in front of his face.

"Come on... put 'em up!"

He moved in towards the black man, in a half-crouch. Alarmed, the man stood up. Arthur moved back a bit.

"Come on..." he said again, remembering how Joe Frazier used to look when he was fighting, and trying to hunch his shoulders in the same manner. "Come on...."

The man didn't seem to get the idea at all. Maybe he'd never seen Joe Frazier. All he could say was, "But... I...."

"Come on," said Arthur. Then, changing tacks—"Out!"

He grabbed the man by the arm and pulled him, almost without resistance, across the room and out into the entrance hall. He was pushing him out of the front door when Fiona emerged from the bedroom.

"What are you doing?" She sounded incredulous.

"Throwing out your boyfriend," Arthur said curtly.

"He's the taxi driver."

"I don't care if he's... ah... taxi driver..." Arthur froze. He let his arms drop to his sides. One ached slightly. He wondered if he'd pulled a muscle. He put his hands in his pockets and looked at the carpet. Faintly he heard Fiona apologizing to the man, and asking him to take the cases downstairs. The man assented, and moved around Arthur in a wide arc before disappearing. Arthur determined not to say a word before Fiona spoke, and, after a long painful silence, she did.

"I didn't mean it to happen this way. I wanted to be gone by the time you came home."

Arthur couldn't resist the sarcasm. "Oh, yes… well, that would have been much better, I agree. Then I could have spent the next forty-eight hours wondering where you might be."

"I was going to leave this note." She held out a folded piece of paper, and Arthur took it.

"Oh, great," he said, without reading it. "What does it say? 'Dear Arthur, I'm leaving you, your dinner's in the oven'? Something traditional like that?"

Fiona looked at him with a hint of bitterness. Then she turned and walked into the bedroom. Arthur followed her, reading aloud from the note. He used a high-pitched, tedious preaching voice.

"Dear Arthur, I'm sorry but I have decided to leave you. I just can't stand jiving with you anymore…."

He realized what he'd read, and looked at the words again.

"Jiving? Oh, no—living." He read on. "You're just not the man I married. Don't forget to water the plants." He looked up at her. "Is that all?"

Fiona didn't reply. She was carefully folding a nightdress and packing it. Arthur waved the note under her nose. "Is that all?" he repeated.

"Mmmm?" She looked at the note. "Oh—I didn't sign it." She took it from him, took a pen out of his pocket, signed the note carefully, then gave him both pen and note back again.

Arthur thrust the note into his pocket. "You just can't leave like this," he told her.

"I can."

"You can? But I love you."

"I don't love you, Arthur."

This was awful. She couldn't have actually said that. She'd never said it before. Not even during bad rows. But now she had said it. She didn't love him. Arthur began to babble.

"All right, you don't love me, not the best basis for a marriage, granted, but you must feel something for me."

"No, I mustn't." Fiona strode out of the bedroom into the sitting room. Arthur scuttled after her.

"Why not?" he whined. Then suddenly he knew. "There's someone else, isn't there!"

"Yes."

"Don't deny it."

"I'm not."

She wasn't. She wasn't denying it. Arthur felt like he was drowning.

"You mean… there *is* someone else?"

"*Yes.*" She almost shouted.

"Oh, yes." Arthur forced a blasé note into his voice. "I had an idea something like this was going on. Started just over a month ago, didn't it?"

"About two years, yes."

"Two years?" Two years. And never for a moment had he dreamed, not a hint, not a sign, not a mention that there could possibly be anyone! Two years!

He had to know: "What's so special about this… er, what did you say his name was?"

"I didn't."

"Loaded with money, is he?"

"No."

So it wasn't for cash. "Obviously younger."

"No."

So it wasn't for youth. In that case there was only one thing it could be for. "Bit of an animal in bed, then?"

"No," said Fiona, looking him straight in the eye. "No, he's just more fun." And she walked out of the sitting room and into the hall.

"Fun, eh?" Arthur chased after her. He had something to go on at last. "What does he do? Wear a funny hat and Wellington boots and leap on you from the top of the wardrobe?"

"No. Neither does he come to bed in his underpants, smoking a pipe, to finish *The Times* crossword before wham-bam-goodnight-ma'am."

The cab driver reappeared. He'd probably overheard every word. But Arthur tried to cover up, for Fiona's sake. And his.

"Well, darling, have a nice time visiting your sick uncle."

He had the distinct impression that he wasn't fooling anyone.

Fiona pointed to the last two cases. "Just these two now."

Arthur tried a last appeal. "I want you to stay."

The man looked at him and put the cases down. Fiona did not respond.

"All right, then." Arthur gave up. "If you insist on going off with your poor elderly comedian...."

The man picked up the cases and made for the door. "... then I won't stand in your way," Arthur continued. He stepped back away from Fiona, and into the path of the taxi driver, who shied like a horse. Fiona walked to the door.

"You're right," Arthur called after her. "It can't be much fun for you, living here in this central-heated, fully carpeted luxury flat with a balcony overlooking

Regent's Park."

Fiona turned, just outside the door. "There's more to it than that," she told him.

"True, there's the freezer, the washing machine, the car, the Continental holidays, the expensive stunted Japanese trees lounging around the place."

But at that moment Fiona reached in, grabbed the door knocker, and slammed the door shut. Arthur rushed to it and tore it open. Fiona and the man were standing at the lift. Trapped!

"Oh, that's very clever," Arthur told their backs. "We can all slam doors."

And to prove it, he too slammed the door with a flourish. The effect was rather spoiled when, to get back into the flat, he had to find his keys and unlock the thing, but after a moment of fumbling he managed it, and once again slammed the door behind him.

This time the thunderous crash had a new note to it. Puzzled, Arthur turned, and examined the door. A jagged crack now ran in and around the lower hinge. Swearing, he tried the door. It was stiff now, and squeaked, and the bottom dug into the hall carpet. Arthur swore again, then went through the sitting room and out onto the balcony.

Down below him. the black taxi driver appeared with the final cases and made his way toward a taxi in the forecourt. Just behind him came Fiona.

Arthur racked his brains for some suitable epithet to shout at them. All he could think of was "Good riddance!" and that was pathetic. He looked wildly about, and then inspiration struck! Hanging from the top of the balcony door was an iron bracket, in which squatted one of the hateful dwarf Jap trees. That would do. That would do very well.

Arthur lifted the plant out of its holder, then ran

forward to lean over the balcony rail.

"Fiona!"

She stood by the taxi, but didn't turn.

"Fiona!"

Still no reaction, although the driver had stopped and was watching Arthur.

"Darling," he tried. "Mrs. Harris!" And then in desperation, "Miss Eweing!"

Fiona made just the slightest movement with her head. That was good enough for Arthur.

"You forgot something," he yelled. He held the wretched tree high above his head, so that bits of soil ran down into his sleeve.

"Your bonsai tree! It's decided that it's... a kamikaze tree!"

With a whoop, he bowled the thing in a great triumphant arch, high up and out and down to a shattering splatt!! in the forecourt.

He had deliberately kept the thing away from the cab. He made sure there was no real danger to Fiona and the driver, and indeed the cab was now moving out into the road. But then Arthur saw that he had nearly brained a woman walking across the forecourt from the opposite direction. As it was, she was spattered with earth from the thing.

Horrified, Arthur turned to rush down and see her. After two strides he ran straight into the iron bracket.

Two

Three-quarters of an hour later Arthur himself was leaving the forecourt. He was on foot, and en route for the pub.

He still felt a little shaky. He'd given himself a considerable bang on the bracket. He'd found himself on his knees in the balcony door, his eyes were fuzzy, and the bells of hell were going dingalingaling inside his skull. He'd practically been knocked out, he realized with some pride. That had never happened to him before. In imitation of James Bond, who always did this sort of thing when he "came to" after a period of unconsciousness, he shook his head to clear it. It was a bad idea. Arthur's head nearly fell off.

As calmly as he could, he waited until the worst of the pounding stopped. Then he got up and, very cautiously, holding his head as level as possible, he left the flat and took the lift down to the ground floor.

The lift doors opened. There, facing him, was the woman he had nearly decapitated. Arthur looked her full in the face, ready to apologize, and found that, magically, his headache had gone.

"Oh, er... are you all right? I'm... er... terribly sorry... about the tree...."

As he stuttered out his apology, Arthur found himself staring at her with feelings of unbridled lust. There was something about her that put all his pleasure-centres into overdrive. She had a kind of sexual sparkle that pushed the gloom of the previous hour into a far corner of his mind. She had crisp silver-gold curls framing a slightly squashed little face, and blue eyes which actually danced. She wore trousers which at the lower end were tucked into calf-length leather boots, and at the upper end were tucked into whatever creases came naturally. She looked pert, personable, and just possibly available. And she looked as if nothing could ever make her sad or stop her smiling. Arthur was willing to bet that she had periods with as much fuss as other women have manicures.

He waffled on: "About the tree… I was throwing it at my wife… that is…."

She stopped him there. "What did she throw at you?" American accent, Arthur noted without surprise.

"Just a few home truths," he said, vaguely.

She came close to him, took a tissue from her bag, reached up and dabbed at his forehead.

"Mmmm." She sounded doubtful. "One of them hit you."

Arthur realized two facts simultaneously. One, that he had gashed his forehead on that bracket. Two, that she was wearing the most blatantly erotic perfume he'd ever sniffed.

As she dabbed, Arthur saw a movement over her shoulder. It was the awful caretaker, coming in from outside with a fussy little dustpan-and-brush. Cortège for a bonsai tree.

"It needs a plaster," said the woman. "I've got…."

"I've got some, thanks," Arthur told her.

"All, well… if there's… anything else you need… cup of sugar or something… my name's Angie, I'm in flat five. First floor."

Arthur swallowed. His mouth was dry. "Right," he croaked.

She nodded. Was there just the suggestion of a wink? Then she moved past him, and started up the steps to the first floor. Arthur watched her go. Or to be more accurate, he watched her behind. It was a beauty. A real Class-A, Number One, Golden-Rose-Of-Montreux-type bottom. A classic.

But as he watched, Arthur became aware of a curious sound. A sort of sucking noise. Curious, he looked around. Standing slightly to one side, behind him, was the awful caretaker. The man still held the pan from which protruded bits of dead bonsai tree. He too was watching Angie's incomparable anatomy, and there was a look of lechery on his face which, Arthur feared, mirrored his own. And as Arthur looked at him, the awful caretaker turned and his eyes met Arthur's, and he gave one of those friendly intimate little nods that manly chaps exchange when they share a secret.

Arthur felt as if he'd been discovered in some nameless act of immorality in a public convenience. He pushed desperately at the lift button. Thankfully, the doors opened at once, and he escaped.

As soon as he closed the door of his own flat behind him, the headache returned. Feeling slightly sick, Arthur wandered through the sitting room and into the bathroom. He tried to put his forehead under the cold tap, but the trendy modern avocado basin was far too shallow, and his efforts just jammed the cut against the tap, undoing all the good work done by American Angie's tissues, and causing a renewed spring of his life force to spurt down the plughole. Cursing, he grabbed a handful of white fluffy towel, and buried his face in it. He breathed long and low, and he could hear his heart thudding. He hated cutting himself.

Eventually the bleeding stopped. Arthur sat on the loo for a while, wondering what to do next. Then he got up and opened the medicine cupboard. He remembered that this was where Fiona kept the Pill.

Sometimes he remembered to ask her if she'd taken it, and she always had. Fiona was like that. Well, she'd taken it all right today, too. She'd taken the bloody lot. He wondered which man would now be enjoying her infertility.

He looked for an Elastoplast. There was a red tin. He opened it. It was full of paperclips. Paperclips in the medicine cupboard?

Arthur threw the things on the floor. Typical. A man is bleeding, and the Elastoplast tin is full of paperclips. Typical. It was Fiona's job to organize things like this. What else did she do all day? She didn't go to work. Couldn't she find enough time just to slip out and buy a new tin of the stuff? What did she do with all those endless hours every day? Probably watched all those women's programmes that told them what to do with their spare time. Only they haven't *got* any spare time left after watching them.

He walked back into the sitting room, and across to the imitation Queen Anne desk. In a drawer reserved for wrapping materials and string, he found what he was looking for. Sellotape. He then found the kitchen scissors, and snipped off a strip some three inches long. Then, back in the bathroom, he examined the gash on his forehead. It was vertical. Therefore a horizontal plaster should hold it together. Delicately he applied the Sellotape. It stuck.

Arthur admired the resulting effect in the mirror. On the whole, he thought, it was a pity the Sellotape was the sort specially designed for Christmas wrapping.

But by the time he had descended in the lift once again, and was striding out across the forecourt, Arthur had forgotten that his forehead was decorated with a strip of redbreasted robins, Santas, and Christmas trees.

He was thinking of a cheerful pub, of people, laughter, company, something to take his mind off things. He was thinking of a drink.

When you drive a cab you have good days and you have bad days. For Gary Manners this was turning out to be a bad day.

He was having the kind of aggravation that he did not need.

First there was the loonie in the flat. The husband who wanted to fight. The big boxer. The Great White Hopeless.

It seemed the guy thought that Gary and his wife had been having a thing. That would be a funny story to tell when he got home. Only Gary wouldn't tell it, because Gary's wife was so jealous, she'd *believe* that Gary and that woman had been really at it, and she wouldn't just put up her fists and prance around, she'd fetch him one with the broom.

Well, that was the first thing. And then, when they get outside, there's the guy throwing plants at them from his balcony. Thank God his aim was no better than his fighting. Once again, not a patch on Gary's wife.

But now he gets the woman in his cab, and it's her turn to go to pieces.

"Waterloo Station. Fast."

Okay, Waterloo it is. No problem. "Eighty pence."

"No, I don't want Waterloo. I want King's Cross."

Okay, King's Cross it is....

"King's Cross? No... take me to Victoria."

Victoria....

"The air terminal."

The air terminal.

"The airport."

The airport.

And all the time she's flitting about in the back like a moth around a lightbulb. Head in hands, then staring out of the window, then eyes shut head back, then chewing the nails, then....

.... and finally: "I know where I want to go now."

And thank the Lord, she does. The address was in Camden Town. Garry pulls into the kerb, and out she jumps and rings the bell. The door is opened by a real Mr. Aftershave, who looks at her like she's from Vernons Pools.

"Fiona!" he says. "How super to see you."

"And you," she says, voice wavering.

Smoothiechops bends over and kisses her cheek, and then the woman frightens him and Gary by bursting into tears and rushing indoors.

It looks like Gary is going to be free of her at last, so he hoicks out all the cases and carries them up to the door and drops them at Actionman's feet. The second thing he drops is a very heavy hint.

"The lady hasn't paid."

"Oh—how much is it?"

"Twenty-two pounds fifty-eight."

That takes the shine off Dreamboat's style. "What?" he says. Then, "Where's she just come from, the West Indies?"

Now that's one real aggravation about being a black taxi driver. Everyone thinks that line is new and original and fresh. "Two pound? Where've we been, Sambo? The West Indies?" Ha ha, very funny.

But Gary can cope. He just gives wonderboy the silent routine. The gimlet eye. The beware stare. The George Foreman face-off.

Sunshine folds like the *Daily Mirror,* and gets out

his wallet. At which gesture Gary explains about Waterloo and King's Cross and Victoria and the air terminal and the airport, and then Superstud shuts him up by dumping a load of cash in his hand and disappearing inside.

So Gary sits in his cap and counts the cash, and it comes to twenty-two pounds fifty-eight, plus ten pence tip.

When you drive a cab you have good days and you have bad days. Roll on, repatriation.

Tony's flat was, in his opinion, a work of art. It had to be art, because it cost so much. It was undoubtedly the poshest pulling pad that nature, technology and the earning power of a youngish criminal lawyer could devise. Tony's super stereo produced sounds of pure gold, manufactured as they were from Tony's pure gold. Tony's gorgeous furry rugs came guaranteed to tickle that most erogenous of zones, the sole of the foot—providing of course one took one's shoes off first. Concealed lighting winked with sly significance. And the drinks cabinet contained enough liquor to launch a thousand hips. As a posh pulling pad, how could it fail? Tony himself believed that it should be written up in *Ideal Home*—perhaps as an example of a bachelor flat that could wreck many an ideal home.

But as yet it wasn't getting to Fiona.

When he'd finished dealing with the taxi driver, Tony found her standing helplessly in the centre of his velvet trap, weeping copious tears. She then insisted on throwing herself into his arms, at the same time greatly upping the water rate. Skillfully he adjusted her handkerchief between her face and himself, thus saving his new fie from becoming a total washout.

He knew conversation would start soon. It always did. So mentally he prepared his full range of voices, tones and characterizations. The right words, said the right way, could work wonders.

First, the chummy big brother—"Tell Tony all about it."

"I've walked out on Arthur."

Desperately sympathetic—"Oh, my poor darling." This, of course, re-opened the floodgates.

"I don't really know why," Fiona sobbed. "I'd just had enough of him.... I lied to him. I told him..." more sobs "... I told him that there was someone else. And had been for two years."

"Oh." Careful disinterest—"I hope he doesn't think... er... that it's me... or anything."

"Of course not." Finally, thankfully, she broke away. "Oh, I'm sorry, I'm putting you to a lot of trouble."

"Nonsense." Time for alcohol. He rapidly mixed up vodka, bitters, limejuice, ice. Always a winner.

"Not too much, Tony."

Warm, brown, comforting—"It'll help you relax."

"I shouldn't have come here."

Manly, strong, confident—"It's natural that you should come straight here... well, almost straight here. I am Arthur's best friend."

Fiona gave him a weak smile. Time for the knife between the shoulderblades.

"... in spite of the selfish, thoughtless, deplorable, hurtful, shoddy...."

"Oh, he's not that bad."

"You're fantastic!" Boyish, youthful, admiring—"Unbelievable!"

"What?"

And now a reminder of his own personal stature:

"You only see the good in people. You'd make a great defence lawyer. I've got a case now in which the only good thing I can say for the defendant is that he once gave fifty blankets to Oxfam."

"That should carry some weight," said Fiona.

"Not really." Chance here to demonstrate sense of humour:

"He was arrested a week later for stealing four hundred blankets from a warehouse."

Fiona laughed.

"That's better." More alcohol. "I'll top you up." He took Fiona's glass and moved back to the drinks cabinet.

"No more, please. I must be going."

"Going where?"

"I don't know… but…."

Dominant, generous—"You're staying here."

"Oh, I couldn't."

"Why not?" Reassuring— "Got the spare room. I'll just open the window and air it a bit."

Leaving Fiona with her topped-up tranquillizer, Tony slipped into his small spare room. It was immaculate. The bed was neatly made, the rug square, the bedside table polished, the pictures square, the bedside lamp glowing softly.

It took Tony just three minutes to stuff the bedclothes in a drawer, push the bed against the wall, roll the mattress up and stuff it in a cupboard, ditto with the carpet, remove the bedside light and the main light shade, drop the pictures in a handy drawer, and spread some newspaper about on the floor.

Fiona came to the door. "There's no need to… oh!"

Tony produced a charming grin of the embarrassed clumsy male. "I forgot it's being redecorated next week. But I can soon make it comfortable."

He'd only rehung one picture when Fiona stopped him.

"Oh, please don't, it's not necessary."

"You're right." Worth a try right now. "You can sleep in my bed."

Fiona's reaction was immediate, definite, negative. Oh, well… time for splendid self-sacrificing gesture:

"*I'll* sleep on the sofa."

It was a good pub. Very Londony pub, too, with one of those high ornate wooden partitions down the centre of the serving area, and a long wide, curving bar. A good bar, too. Wooden and highly polished, with a gleaming brass footrail. Even the stools were of superior quality. Firm. Padded. Easily tilted, so that the drinker can rest his elbows on the highly polished bar, hook his toes in the gleaming brass footrail, and stare at the high ornate wooden partition, and… think.

And… drink.

Arthur had spent the evening doing much of both. The tide of the night's custom had ebbed and flowed around him, and not disturbing him from one solitary moment in the pursuit of his goal. He sat in a small island of empty crisp packets. The tenth large gin and tonic sat before him. The other nine sat inside him. Tonight, he felt, would go on forever.

Suddenly his glass was empty again. He waved to the barman.

"Could I have…."

But the barman was already pouring it. He placed it in front of Arthur, and deducted some coins from the pile on the bar. Arthur fished in his drink until he captured the slice of lemon. This he added to a pile of lemon slices on the bar.

"A few more of these," he said proudly, "and I will have re-built a lemon."

"Yeah." The barman was a cynic. "But you'll have collapsed."

Arthur took no notice. Instead he picked up a two-pence piece from his change and lurched over to the phone. Three rings, and the call was answered.

"Tony?" said Arthur, when the pips stopped. "It's Arthur."

"Arthur?" Tony might never have heard the name in his life.

"Harris!"

Something funny happened at the other end of the line. Arthur thought he heard another voice, muffled. Then he thought he'd been cut off. Then Tony came back on the line.

"Arthur! How are you?"

"Depressed."

"Oh, really?"

Arthur frowned. Tony sounded almost pleased. He tried again. "Terrible. Fiona has walked out on me."

"Great!"

"Great?" Tony had gone barmy, that was the only explanation.

"Tony, she has *left* me."

"Couldn't agree more, old boy."

"Tony," said Arthur, with a sudden flash of inspiration. "Tony, are you pleased?"

"Yes!"

"Me, too."

Tony's laugh crackled down the phone.

"She's left me," Arthur told him again. "Walked out. On our *tenth* wedding anniversary."

"Really?"

"Oh, yes." Tony had been best man. "Thanks for the table lamp."

"Don't mention it."

Arthur felt tears of nostalgia and self-pity behind his eyelids. After all, Tony was his best, his oldest and closest friend. It was good to have him to talk to.

"I mean, you're my closest friend," he told him, "and I can't even begin to explain how I feel... the bottom's just fallen out of my life.... I don't know what to do."

"Great idea!"

Good grief, the man *was* pissed.

"Well, er... thank God I've got you to talk to...."

"Absolutely." Tony sounded more brisk than ever. "I'll give you a ring tomorrow."

"Tomorrow? I...."

"Cheers, old boy." And the phone clicked in Arthur's ear.

"What did he say?" asked Fiona.

Tony knew what was needed. A really unsettling sense of disappointment. "He's fine. Great form. He said that you'd gone, and he thinks it's for the best. He's determined to enjoy life and hopes you're doing the same."

And before she could start crying again, he gave her a reassuring hug. She felt good. Carefully he kept his hands under control. He'd been waiting for ten years to have a feel of Fiona's bum. He could wait a little longer.

Three

"Time, gentlemen, please," said the barman.

Arthur, who had come to regard the barman as a friend, perhaps a comrade, maybe even a brother, felt betrayed. He decided to ignore what the man had said.

"Same again, please."

The barman came and stood facing him. Arthur thought what a kind face he had. It reminded him of a Labrador his parents had owned. He thought he might tell the barman that, and then he thought he wouldn't bother.

"Sorry," said the barman. "It's time, and you haven't finished your last drink."

What? Oh, no, of course he hadn't. Arthur tilted his stool forward, picked up the half-full glass of gin and tonic, and drained it in one.

And then the most remarkable thing happened. The whole room turned on its side.

Arthur didn't understand how that could have happened, but the barman obviously did, because he came and set the room back the right way up, and helped Arthur to his feet. Naturally Arthur had fallen on his back, because anyone would if the room fell over, too, so he didn't bother to apologize for doing it, but there was one thing he was proud of.

"I didn't break the glass," he boasted.

"True," the barman acknowledged. "But you did break the stool, the table and an ashtray."

The barman seemed to understand Arthur, and as a gesture of appreciation for his support, Arthur put his arms around the man. Unsteadily, they made for the door.

"Are you married?" Arthur asked.

"No," said the barman, with a certain amount of caution.

"Lucky sod!" said Arthur, and stumbled out into the night.

Arthur knew that the brisk walk in the cold night air from pub to flat would sober him up and, sure enough, as he staggered across the forecourt to the flats, he was more drunk than he'd been in ten years. The brisk walk had started his heart pumping like a piston, sending alcohol-laden blood rushing along his arteries like a never-ending commuter train, while down in his stomach the last gin and tonic was queueing up to push its way through the stomach wall and join in the rush. He was drunker now than he had been in the pub, and he would be drunker still.

But Arthur also knew, with the calm trusting faith that always comes after the eighth g. and t., that all he had to do was concentrate and everything would be all right. If he could focus his thoughts with sufficient power on every single task that now faced him, then he would perform with skill and dexterity. To test the theory, he concentrated on walking in an exact straight line across the forecourt to the door of the flats. To his infinite pleasure, he did it, even throwing in a slight chicane to avoid Mrs. Thompson's Pekinese's evening deposit, which lay glinting slightly in the street lights.

And so Arthur arrived at the front door.

Now a greater degree of concentration was required. The door was locked. Therefore keys were required to open the door. Keys were in the trouser pocket. Arthur found the trouser pocket at the second attempt, the keys at the first attempt. So far, very good. But then suddenly the ludicrous side of the situation struck him. How incredibly funny that he should be required to concentrate so strongly! How impossible to hold up a keyring containing car keys, desk key, flat door keys, freezer keys, suitcase keys, AA keys, old flat keys, office keys and cycle padlock keys, not to mention at least eight keys the purpose of which he had long forgotten, and from these to select the one key necessary for opening the front door. Totally impossible, totally laughable.

The keys rattled impotently against the glass panel of the door, and Arthur giggled.

But his enjoyment of the funny side of it all came to a sudden halt, because something was happening on the other side of the door which he didn't like. Coming out of his little cubby hole, switching on the main light, and advancing towards the door with his own unique gait which Arthur had once described as a "shuffling strut," was the awful caretaker.

Concentration, Arthur told himself fiercely. Concentration was the answer. The awful caretaker must not know, must not even suspect, that he'd been out drinking. That would be too shaming. Artfully, he held his bunch of keys up to the light, and pretended to be looking for the right one. He found this quite easy to pretend, because he actually was looking for the right one. He assumed a nonchalant, easy-going expression. The important thing was that the caretaker should not suspect for one instant that he was drunk.

The caretaker opened the door. "Mr. Harris?" he queried. "You drunk?"

Arthur ignored him. Such a remark, following Arthur's extensive preparations to prove he was *not* drunk, only revealed the man's stupidity.

The caretaker stood back, holding the door open so that Arthur could enter. But once again Arthur was too smart for him. He wasn't going to be caught out like that.

"Hang on," he muttered, and then… "Alia!" as he finally found the right key. Carefully he moved forward into the open doorway, found the keyhole in the door, inserted the key, wriggled it about convincingly, then withdrew it, and pocketed the set of keys.

That would show the awful caretaker that he wasn't too drunk to open a door. Ha! No wonder the man was staring.

Arthur set out to walk to the lift. First he walked to the left-hand wall of the hall. Then across to the right-hand wall. And then back to the left-hand wall. He was forced to concede that the alcohol was making him a little unsteady.

This would have been more shaming had not the awful caretaker been equally unsteady. He too seemed to be staggering back and forth across the hall, in exact time with Arthur. Once he even put a hand on Arthur's arm, presumably to hold himself up. The man was drunk. It was a disgrace.

They reached the lift. Arthur allowed the caretaker to press the button, partly because that was his job, and partly because Arthur had forgotten you have to do that.

There was a short silence while they waited. Then the caretaker said: "Bit… er… nippy out tonight."

This was Arthur's opportunity—the opportunity finally to crush the man, and establish his own infinite intellectual superiority, with one retort, one flashing incisive remark, one totally unanswerable shaft of brilliance. Arthur opened his mouth, waiting eagerly to see what it was he would say.

He was still waiting when the lift came. So he shut his mouth and got in. The lift doors closed.

Arthur raised a finger to press the button for his

floor. Then, inexplicably, at least to Arthur at that moment, the finger moved down and pressed the button for the first floor. The lift moved hardly at all before it stopped, and the doors opened. Arthur found himself out on the landing, facing a strange flat door.

Number five. American Angie's.

Arthur had a momentary qualm. Perhaps, after the long evening in the pub, he wasn't quite his normal desirable self. He ran his tongue over his teeth and wondered about his breath. Would it smell of gin? He straightened his tie, ran a hand through his hair, tried to see himself reflected in the brass plate on Angie's door. Something white and distorted stared back at him. For a moment he felt rather ill.

Arthur rang the bell.

Of course he had to wait for a few moments, and this proved a little difficult, because on however-many gin and tonics you can stand up while you've got something to do, something to concentrate on, like combing your hair with your fingers, but when you've got nothing to do except stand there, you can't stand there. You sway, and you need to lean against the wall. Arthur leaned against the wall. It was, he thought, a typical Robert Mitchum pose, all casual, lazy and cool. He put a Robert Mitchum sneer on his face. If he'd been wearing a coat he'd have turned up the collar. As it was, he thought it might look funny if he turned up the collar of his suit.

The door opened. Angie stood there. She no longer wore the trousers. Now she had on a long filmy robe, the kind of thing advertised in *The Sunday Times,* which seemed to be held together only by a cord around the waist. She looked fabulous. She seemed surprised.

"Oh," she said. Half surprise, half question.

"Hello, again," said Arthur, winningly.

Angie said nothing to this. She just looked a little less surprised, a little more questioning. Arthur plunged on.

"Your doorbell!"

"What?"

"It was just... standing there... not doing anything... er... so I rang it."

Now that was pretty good, Arthur told himself. Pretty good indeed. The doorbell wasn't doing anything, so I rang it. Pretty neat. Nice one. By now Angie should be laughing, maybe putting her hand on his arm, bringing him inside. But she wasn't.

Angie said: "Oh."

Arthur tried another approach. "You... mentioned a drink earlier." She hadn't, she'd said a cup of sugar, but what the hell?

Angie smiled. "Oh, yes. Are you alone?"

Arthur nodded. "And you?"

"Yes."

"Well... if I come in, then neither of us will be alone."

That was pretty good, too. How many years was it since he'd last chatted his way into a girl's flat? Too many. Yet the old methods still worked. The old technique wasn't rusty. Yes, it really was working.

Angie gave him a sympathetic smile. "Come on, then." She stood aside. Arthur pushed himself away from his supporting wall, swayed for a moment, then lurched into the flat. Angie shut the door behind him.

She made a slight gesture with her hand. "Excuse the mess."

Arthur smiled at her. He felt in total command. There was a lot of R. Mitchum in his voice when he spoke: "You look fine to me."

"I meant…."

"In fact, you look bloody great."

Arthur's pleasure in his own verbosity reached a new peak. That too had been incredibly apt. Tonight he was at his best. Perhaps Angie wasn't that amused by what he'd said so far, but he was certainly amusing himself. He followed her into her sitting room. It was nice—expensive, cool, straight out of Heal's. Arthur felt at home.

Angie turned to him: "Would you rather have a coffee?"

"Than what?"

"Than a drink?"

Arthur fumbled for a moment. "Oh, yes… er… no. A drink."

"Brandy?"

And here it was again—another chance to be incredibly suave and witty.

"Why not a brandy? It makes you…." And then he stopped. Perhaps not. Not yet, anyway.

"Makes you…?" prompted Angie, pouring two large brandies.

"Makes you… drunk if you have enough of it," Arthur finished lamely. He took his glass. "Thanks—cheers."

"Sit down," Angie invited.

Arthur looked around, chose a broad leather chair, and sank back into it with a sigh of relief. He felt he was floating on air.

Angie sank gracefully to sit cross-legged on the floor, the filmy gown floating around her like a veil. Looking at her from his perch on the chair, Arthur felt awkward and leggy. Gently, head swimming a little, he eased himself out of the seat, and squatted on the carpet. A stabbing pain flashed through one knee. The other one cracked like a chicken bone.

"I find it more comfortable than the sofa," Angie told him.

"So it is." Arthur shifted position, and for one agonizing millisecond he sat on his keys. He shifted again and eventually found a pose that was only moderately unbearable. He managed a smile.

Angie was looking at him with an intensity he hadn't seen before.

"You're...."

"Pissed?" Arthur prompted.

"Well, that as well...." she agreed.

"Been celebrating," Arthur explained. "Some good news and some bad news."

He could make this really funny, he thought. This would slay her.

"Oh?" she asked.

"Yes—today is my tenth wedding anniversary, and today my wife left me."

Angie wasn't slain. In fact, she didn't laugh at all. She just repeated "Oh," but in a different tone of voice.

Arthur continued the joke: "The funny thing is, I don't know which is the good news and which is the bad."

This struck him as so incredibly amusing that he didn't wait to see if Angie found it the same. Instead he flung his head back and roared with laughter. It wasn't a wise move. He tipped backwards completely, toppling into a chair which slid across the floor. Totally out of balance, Arthur crashed back with it, and finished flat on his back on the carpet.

He stared up at the ceiling. It swayed. He shut his eyes. The entire floor revolved. He hastily opened his eyes again. Gradually the universe came to rest.

Angie was on her knees by his side, her squashy

little face concerned and sympathetic. He felt strangely warm towards her.

"Are you all right?" he asked.

She blinked. "Yes."

As she knelt there, Arthur became aware that his first supposition about her robe had been correct. It *was* only held together at the waist. Because now a long slim slender thigh had emerged. Arthur gazed at it. It was incredible. A piece of sensual perfection. He looked up at Angie, and knew she had been watching him watching her.

She put her arms under his, lifting him, and together they staggered to their feet. He found his arms around her waist, and dropped them to his sides. But she kept hers around him, her hands gripping the upper parts of his arms. This, he discovered, further loosened her gown. It billowed out now in front. He looked down. Her breasts were small and far apart. They were brown. He wondered if she sunbathed in the nude. He couldn't see her nipples.

He looked back into Angie's eyes. She was smiling again, warm and inviting. He could just sense her body against his.

"You came round here hoping to screw me, didn't you!"

Arthur swallowed. She had actually said "screw." Not even "make love." My God, she was… something! And she was waiting for an answer.

"Er… er… did I? Did I make it so obvious?"

Angie nodded, as if bursting with laughter. "Mmmmm."

Arthur felt terrible. He felt caught out. He felt embarrassed, ashamed and humiliated. He remembered how it had been when he'd been caught in the toilets at school reading *Spick And Span,* and that was how it felt now.

He stuttered: "Oh… sorry… I… I'll have…," and began to turn towards the door.

"What for?"

Arthur turned back, bewildered. "Well… you just…."

She was still standing close to him. Her hands were still on his arms. She smiled brightly up at him.

"It's fine by me," she said.

"What?"

"I'm game." And then she pushed her hips against him, and gave him a brief but unbelievable nudge.

Arthur, knowing he sounded stupid, said: "Now?"

She grinned again. "Why, do you have a particular time when you…."

"No… no. I… er…" Arthur didn't know what he could say to her. He had to say something—anything. Anything but the truth which at that moment he was rapidly recognizing—that he didn't want to. Mentally she was still his ideal wet-dream partner—still a scintillatingly sexy, beautiful female. But physically his body had declared its total disinterest. It had no reaction. It couldn't raise the slightest twitch, the merest flip, the faintest tremble of interest. It was dead from the knees up. The truth was, he didn't want to do it. There were a million things he'd rather do. He'd rather wash the car. He'd rather go to the launderette. He'd rather accept a free lesson as an introduction to a full course of ballroom and Latin-American dancing. He'd rather queue up all night to watch Nottingham Forest. He'd rather take part in a police identification parade and be wrongly identified. He'd rather do anything than make love to Angie. His body didn't want to do it.

He wondered how he was going to tell her.

"Well?" she queried.

"I… just haven't finished my drink."

Angie held up his brandy glass, which had somehow survived his fall. "You have." He had. It was empty.

"Oh, yes… er, yes. Right." Arthur heard his own voice, heavy with insincerity. But Angie didn't seem to notice. Quickly, efficiently, she moved around the room, putting lights out. Arthur stood where he was. He felt awkward. His hands hung limply by his sides—not, he noted grimly, the only things that were hanging limply.

Angie smiled at him. "The bedroom's through there…."

Arthur expressed interest like a seasoned estate agent. "Oh, is it? And the kitchen?"

A shadow crossed Angie's face. "You don't want to do it in the kitchen, do you?"

Briefly, Arthur remembered a moment years ago, when he and Fiona did it in the kitchen, while her parents watched *This Is Your Life* in the other room, and the Marley Tiles played hell with his elbows.

"No… no." He laughed nervously.

"Oh… you're hungry?"

"No… I was just wondering if all these apartments are the same. You see… our kitchen is more like… there… and our bedroom is… well…."

Angie put an end to his wild gestures by coming across, close to him, pressing herself against him, ruffling his hair. Just for a moment her other hand caressed his bottom. Arthur jumped.

Her voice was softer now. "It's always the quiet ones, isn't it!"

"Is it?" asked Arthur, dazed.

Angie took his hand, and led him like a pet dog across the room, and into her bedroom.

"I'll just do my teeth." She turned and went back out into the sitting room, leaving him standing in the middle of the fluffy off-white carpet. He felt totally alone.

The room was a celebration of femininity. It was all soft edges, gentle colours, sweet smells. Arthur felt gross and sweaty, he hardly dared move. In the background he dimly heard Angie brushing her teeth. She did it in a typically American way—swift hard strokes, ultra-efficient. He wondered if she made love the same way. Swallowing, he examined a pile of underclothes hanging from a delicate white chair. He picked up a garment. It was the ultimate in sexual underwear—a collection of lace, frills and holes in the shape of panties. Loose, impractical, delicious. He rubbed his fingers against the satiny material, and just for a brief moment something stirred in the undergrowth.

And then, with a hawk and a spit, Angie audibly ejected used toothpaste into a basin, and for Arthur, everything went dead again.

Angie's smile when she returned was a testament to regular American-style teeth brushing. She affected surprise.

"Oh—you're still dressed."

"I... haven't brushed my teeth yet." Good thinking, Arthur.

"Oh. Go ahead."

Angie shrugged her shoulders, her arms stretched behind her. The robe slid down her arms, off and away to a heap on the floor. For a moment Arthur looked at her. Then she turned, her bottom twinkling at him, and she was in bed, under the white duvet.

Arthur cleared his throat. "Right then. I'll just nip up to my place and get my toothbrush."

Angie laughed. "Are you kidding? There's a throwaway guest one in a packet to the left of the washbasin."

"Right."

Toothbrush or no toothbrush, nothing was going to stop Arthur now. He walked briskly out of the bedroom, closing the door behind him. Across the sitting room he could see the open door to the bathroom. A yellow suite. Yuk! He began walking towards it, then veered sharply off to the right, leaning into the curve as he went, until he came to the open door to the entrance hall. Through he went, and up to the main door. Carefully he turned the latch, then slipped through like a burglar, and closed the door silently behind him.

Then like an athlete he sprinted up the stairs. Two flights, three, breath sobbing, until he found himself outside his own front door. A quick fumble with keys, and he was in. Home. Safe.

He stood inside the dark hall, panting, listening. He heard the distant hum of traffic, the closer hum of the fridge in the kitchen. He wondered what Angie would do. Take it in her stride, he guessed. Shrug, smile, forget it. He'd probably confirmed some long-standing supposition about Englishmen. Or rather, in his case, not standing at all.

He didn't care. The experience had done one thing for him. It had totally cleared his head. He was not drunk. The alcohol had been driven out of his system. He felt calm, in control, undeniably sober. And if he was sober, then he needed a drink.

Without bothering about lights, he strode through his entrance hall, into the sitting room and across to the drinks cabinet. He grabbed a glass in one hand, a bottle in the other. He unscrewed, poured, drank long and deep.

It was Crème de Menthe.

Four

Arthur woke up so fast he nearly fell off the sofa. One moment he was deep in the darkest of dark sleeps. The next he was awake, and hurting, and there was no way that he could go back to sleep. He was wide awake, and suffering.

His first thought was to wonder why he'd slept on the couch. He could have made the bed, surely. It was just across the room and through the door. Birds twittered outside the window. Engines revved. People banged things. He wondered what time it was.

Arthur then thought that perhaps he should try to move, and he made a gentle attempt to change his position. It was not wise. His head was tucked into the crook of one elbow, with his face pressed against the brocade of the sofa back, and it ached when he tried to move it. He decided to leave it where it was for the time being. His other hand lay in his groin, so he lifted it and grabbed the top of the sofa back for extra support. This done, he felt more confident. Perhaps now he could move his legs. One of these was already resting on the floor. Okay. The question was, where was the other leg? He couldn't feel it at all. For a moment he wondered if it had fallen off. He flexed leg muscles that ought to have been there, and was rewarded with a heavy thumping noise from the far end of the sofa. The leg was there. Totally asleep, but there.

Gripping the sofa securely with his free hand, he swung the dead leg up and over and down to ground level. The heel of the shoe on this leg crashed into the ankle of the other leg. The pain was immediate, and obliterated all other aches and pains. Arthur yelped and shot upright. There was a sharp ripping noise, and a fresh spring of pain in his forehead, where it had been pressed against the sofa, but Arthur didn't care.

Instead he sat, crumpled on the edge of the sofa. One hand reached down to massage his bruised ankle. The other wiped sleep from his eyes. Arthur moaned in his misery.

After a minute or two he began to wonder what that ripping noise had been. He turned, slowly, and looked at the sofa. Sticking to the material was a three-inch strip of blood-stained Christmas Sellotape.

It was at this point that Arthur began to remember the events of the previous day. He had cut his forehead and had used the Sellotape instead of Elastoplast. That was it. Which meant he'd spent the evening in the pub with that on his face. *And* then there'd been that business with the woman Angie, and she hadn't said a word about it. Despite his misery, Arthur spluttered at the thought of it. How Fiona would laugh when she....

Fiona!

She'd left him.

He'd forgotten. For about a minute and a half he had forgotten, and things were as they should be. But now he remembered.

Grimly he got to his feet. The movement toppled the scotch bottle which had been standing by the sofa, and what was left in it now gurgled out onto the carpet. Arthur let it gurgle.

There was a chance, just a chance, only a chance, that she'd come back. That some time during the night she'd realized her mistake, told the other man that it was all over, and caught a taxi home. Perhaps right now she was in there, behind the bedroom door, sound asleep. Perhaps he'd be able to creep into bed with her, and hold her, and....

Arthur limped rapidly across the sitting room and flung open the bedroom door.

The empty bed sneered at him.

Arthur told himself he had been foolish to hope. She had gone. He must accept it. He had nothing of her left.

Well, almost nothing. Arthur sat down on the side of the bed. A pair of tights had somehow escaped in yesterday's frenetic packing session. He picked them up from the floor. They were Fiona's. They must be, they weren't his. Arthur tried to smile, but there was no humour left in him.

He got to his feet and began searching the room for more traces of his wife. Once he began looking, he found plenty.

She'd forgotten her rollers. A set of plastic multi-coloured torture implements, in a transparent plastic bag, tucked away in the bottom of her bedside cabinet. Then he remembered—last Christmas he'd given her a modern set of heated rollers. These were discards. He checked to see that she'd taken the new set. She had.

A hairbrush lay on the dressing table. He saw clearly why she'd left that. It wasn't the kind of implement one took to a lovers' tryst. It was thick with matted hair. Arthur shrugged. No matter, it was Fiona's hair, something of her that still remained, that he would treasure. Perhaps he could get an envelope from the desk, and remove some of the hair from the brush, and keep it for ever and ever. It was a good thought.

He was halfway towards the door when he remembered that this was the hairbrush they had so many fights about, because he liked to use it too. So any hair he collected might be his own.

There was some make-up, abandoned in a top

drawer of the unit. Nothing much. Some tacky little plastic cases, holding dried-up brown-looking gunk. He sat down at Fiona's dressing table, spat in one of the little tubs, worked it with his finger until it began to goo, then spread a bit on his cheek. He examined the result. It still looked muddy.

He wiped it off with tissues. She'd left them too. Now that was unusual. Fiona was a tissue fanatic. On every journey they ever made, the car had to include at least two boxes of the things, otherwise she felt insecure. At home, every waste bin overflowed with the used ones. Arthur never quite knew what she used them all for—especially as she always carried a handkerchief too—but he'd never nerved himself to sort through the discarded tissues to find out. So it was strange that she had left behind a half-empty box. Unless, of course, this lover of hers was also a tissue fanatic. Perhaps at this moment they were sharing a super-strength super-absorbent man-sized maxi-tissue, she drying her eyes at one end of it, and him blowing his nose at the other.

Arthur opened the last drawer in the bedroom unit. It held an opened box of Tampax. That was all. He shut the drawer again. He didn't even want to think about the implications.

The bathroom offered similar proof that the flat had once contained a feminine presence, which had now departed. He found her plastic shower cap.

In the cabinet he found a packet of her nymphet blades. Fiona shaved her legs regularly. Now why had she left them? Perhaps her new lover was a tough back-to-nature type, and for him she would not be smooth and silky, but rough and stubbly. Arthur hoped bitterly that they were both rough and stubbly, and then maybe they'd rasp each other to death.

Then he noticed that, although she'd left some blades, she'd taken her dinky razor.

And her toothbrush.

And face-flannel. And talc. And soap. And shampoo, and....

No. Not quite all her conditioner. On a ledge lay the mangled remains of a conditioner sachet.

With no feeling of being ridiculous, Arthur picked it up. He squeezed his fingers around it, and the last drop of conditioning liquid oozed out onto the palm of his hand. He held the hand up to his face and breathed in deeply.

The scent was unbearable. It was the scent of her hair. As it filled his head, Arthur recaptured Fiona's whole presence, right there in the bathroom. It was if she was standing next to him, as if he could reach out and touch her.

And then the moment was gone. The smell was just a commercial conditioner. Arthur wiped the stickiness away on a blood-stained towel. For the first time he was totally aware of all that he had lost.

He stood for long minutes, feeling the pain.

Then he opened the bathroom cabinet again and took out his own razor. Resolutely he unscrewed it, and removed the blade. He dropped the razor on the floor, then held up the blade and looked at it, while he rationalized the way he felt.

He felt there was nothing left to live for. And when you have nothing left to live for, well... you just have nothing left to live for. So you die. So....

The phone rang.

Arthur jumped. The blade slipped and nicked his finger. Blood fell in the basin, just as it had the day before. Arthur felt slightly sick, and his heart raced. He hated cutting himself.

He stuck his finger in his mouth and sucked. Then, still sucking, he went through into the sitting room and answered the phone.

"Herrough?" said. Arthur. Then he took his finger out of his mouth and tried again. "Hello?"

"Hello, Arthur?"

Good God, it was Fiona! "Fiona?"

"How are you?" Her voice sounded soft, almost distant.

Arthur found that he almost didn't want to talk to her. Things had gone so far....

"You're lucky to have caught me," he told her. "I was just about to... er... depart."

"Oh... are you going away for long?"

"Permanently." He gave himself a ghostly grin.

"Where to?"

"No idea until I get there." Even better.

"I don't understand."

Arthur tired of his little joke. "Sorry, darling. I should explain. I am going to kill myself." Then without pausing, "And how have you been?"

"What did you say?" Fiona was alarmed.

"How have you been?" Arthur repeated seriously. "Seen any good movies lately?"

"Stop it, Arthur," Fiona told him. "You're not serious, are you?"

"Absolutely." Opportunity for another little joke. "I like to know what films you've seen."

"For God's sake, Arthur...." Arthur felt he could see her chin jutting with determination. "You don't really mean you're going to kill yourself."

"Not quite sure how to do it yet," he said, matter-of-factly. "But there's a big jar of pills in the bathroom cabinet. Swallow that lot, no bother."

Now there was relief in Fiona's voice. "They're

aspirins. And anyway, there's only five left."

"It...." Arthur knew it was lame. "It's still three over the recommended dose!"

"You're in a strange mood," Fiona said dismissively. "I'll speak to you tomorrow."

"Oh, holding a seance, are you?" He was suddenly furious that she wouldn't take him seriously, and slammed the phone down.

After a night on his own sofa, Tony was in no mood to exercise his vocal characterizations at that time in the morning. Fiona's excited babble that Arthur was going to kill himself produced a scant response.

"Huh!"

"But I think he means it."

Wearily Tony explained: "He's only saying that to make you feel guilty."

"I *feel* guilty."

"See?"

Arthur stood on the balcony and looked down. It was a long way down—a straight drop to the asphalt. Well, at least he wouldn't get hung up on any spiky bits on the way down, like people do when they jump off churches. Or bounce off protruding rocks, like people do at Avon Gorge. Or crash through hotel awnings, like people do in New York. No, it was a straight clean drop down to the asphalt.

He braced both hands on the rail and half-lifted one foot up onto it. Then he swayed back down again. It was an awkward height. If he climbed on too fast, he'd topple over the edge. Of course, he was going to topple over the edge eventually, anyway. But he needed a moment or two to compose himself before doing it. A moment of calm recollection, he told himself, before taking the plunge. To coin a phrase.

A compromise was easy. The balcony contained two metal garden chairs. Just right for sitting out on summer evenings. Just right, too, for dragging over to the rail, and standing on, and waiting for the right moment. And the right moment was coming, he was sure of it. He wobbled uncertainly on the chair. He put one foot up on the rail. Braced himself. Shut his eyes. Waited for just one more second, and....

"Careful, Mr. Harris!"

Arthur opened his eyes and looked down. The awful caretaker stood in the centre of the forecourt, gazing up at him.

"A window cleaner fell from the floor above you a couple of years ago," the caretaker called.

"Oh, really?" It was difficult to sound non-committal when shouting.

"Broke both his legs and an arm. He was in hospital for three months. Walks with a limp now, and a stick."

Arthur thought about that. He brought his foot back down from the rail, and wobbled slightly on the chair again. Walking with a limp and a stick... he looked up, and saw that Mr. and Mrs. Kemp, whose flat was two floors up and to one side, were both out on their balcony, looking down at him. Well, if he did do it now, at least he'd have an audience of three. But a limp and a stick....

The awful caretaker made another loud enquiry, and into it he put a distillation of his nosiness, his rudeness, his creepiness, his bitchiness, his whole general awfulness:

"What *are* you doing up there, Mr. Harris?"

And Arthur's control, by now only held by a

thread, snapped.

"Minding my own flaming business, which is more than can be said for you...," and at even greater volume, "you nosy snivelling little turd!"

Mr. and Mrs. Kemp nearly fell off their own balcony with shock.

The awful caretaker turned round three times, swinging his arms in an agony of indecision, then stalked off.

And Arthur got down from his chair.

It is simple to dial the Samaritans. You merely look up the number in your telephone directory, S—Z if in London, and dial. Arthur did this, having first fortified and forearmed himself by preparing a very large Pimms.

The phone was answered almost immediately.

"Hello?" said Arthur. "Samaritans?"

The voice at the other end was infinitely gentle. It betrayed a world of compassion. It exuded understanding. And all in one little word—

"Yes."

"I need some help," Arthur told it.

"Yes?"

"You see, I want to kill myself." Arthur was surprised to find that actually saying it made him feel a little embarrassed. Within himself, he'd become quite used to the idea.

"Would you like to talk about it?" asked the nice voice.

"No, I wouldn't. I'd just like to get on with it."

There was the merest fraction of a pause, before the voice got on with it: "What's caused you to feel like this?"

"I said I didn't want to talk about it," Arthur

snapped. "Look, which is the most popular method?"

"Perhaps if we met, we could…."

Good grief, Arthur thought! Where do they get these people? Can't they train them? Surely they can answer a perfectly simple question when it's put to them!

"Just tell me the quickest and least painful way," he insisted.

The voice drew on its bottomless well of pity. "Please… you're probably upset at the moment."

Brilliant! "Yes, and you're making me more upset. Look, just tell me what to do, and I'll get off the line. There may be people who need you trying to get through."

"We have plenty of lines. I think *you* need me."

"I do. But in a different way. I don't want to be stopped. In fact, I need encouragement."

"I can't do that," the voice protested.

"You're bloody useless, then," Arthur bellowed. Then he slammed the phone down on its rest. He'd write to the papers about it, really he would.

Arthur stood at the drinks cabinet, and poured himself a stiff scotch and water. Then light suddenly dawned. Hanging on the wall over the drinks cabinet was a Samurai sword in an ornate sheaf. Sharp, deadly, made for committing the ultimate act.

Ah-so!

Arthur recalled that it had been a wedding present from Fiona's mum. What a suitable gift, he'd remarked at the time. How useful for a young couple just setting up home. It ought to be on all wedding present lists. Electric kettle, tea service, canteen of cutlery, Samurai sword….

But now at last it did have a use. It would kill

him. Perhaps Fiona's mum had thought ahead to this day.

With his own Western idea of Japanese ceremony, Arthur solemnly lifted the sword down. He examined it for a quiet moment. Then put a hand on the handle, the other on the sheaf, and....

The damn thing wouldn't budge.

He changed hands and tried. He put it under his arm and tried. He gripped in between his feet and tried. He pulled it this way and that way, he shook it, he rattled it, he oiled it, he banged it against the wall, and then he tried.

The damn thing wouldn't budge.

Arthur threw it in a corner, and poured another drink. He would kill himself, he vowed. Or die in the attempt.

Five

The metal balcony chair came in useful a second time. It became a metal balcony electric chair.

Arthur was really quite proud of his home-made electric chair. Especially as he had always hated electricity, and never quite understood how it worked. It just showed what a little motivation can do.

The chair now stood in the centre of the sitting room, directly beneath the chandelier-type main light fitting. Two wires led from the chair up to the chandelier, where they were connected with the light fittings. He'd obtained the wires by vandalizing his stereo system. A shame, perhaps—but then, he wouldn't be listening to it again.

He went to the door, and, nerving himself for a bang or a flash or something else electrical, he flicked the light switch. Nothing happened, except that only two of the four chandelier light bulbs lit.

Arthur was pleased. This meant, he deduced, that the current normally powering the two dead bulbs was now coursing through the metal chair. Anyone who sat on the chair would suffer instant electrical death. Excellent. He flicked the switch, turning the current off, then, tentatively at first but bolder when nothing happened, he took hold of the chair and moved it as near to the door as the wires would allow.

Then, with a sense that he'd been through it all before, Arthur composed himself for death.

He took a last look around the room. Saying good-bye to things. As a final thought, he went to the windows and drew the curtains. Then, in the half light, he came back and sat on the electric chair.

All he had to do now was to switch on the current. He leaned forward, stretching out with his fingertips, and he could nearly reach the switch, but not quite, perhaps just one final stretch and….

Bzzzzzzz!

For a moment Arthur thought he had electrocuted himself. Then he realized it was the doorbell buzzing. He got to his feet and went through into the hall, automatically switching on the sitting room lights as he went. In the hall, he opened the front door.

A little man stood there. A strange little man, wearing a leather coat that covered him from neck to toe, a beret pulled low down over his forehead, and motorcycle goggles pushed up on the top of his head. The strangest thing about the man were his eyes. They were bright, like a bird's, and they flicked here and there, in a constant, enquiring, suspicious movement. Now they flicked briefly up at Arthur.

"Odd jobs?" It was a sharp, piping little voice.

"Eh?"

"Odd jobs?"

"Er… not today… um…." Understandably, Arthur had difficulty in dragging his mind back from the contemplation of infinity to the question of odd jobs.

"Right." The little man turned and began to shuffle away. Arthur was disappointed, he felt he wanted to say something else to the man, and he cleared his throat in a conversational sort of way.

"A—ahem."

Back came the man, like a yo-yo. "Odd jobs?" he asked again.

"Er…." Arthur could think of nothing else to say but, "No."

"Right," said the odd job man, with slightly more final emphasis than before, and shuffled off again.

Arthur closed the door, and stood in his hall, indecisive. He felt lonely. And perhaps it might be an idea if....

He whirled around, pulled the door open, and looked out on the landing. The odd job man was just turning the corner by the lift.

Arthur shouted: "I... um...."

Strangely obedient, the odd job man turned once again and shuffled back. "Yeah?"

"I might have something for you to do. Come in."

"Righto."

The man followed Arthur through into the sitting room. Arthur remembered that he'd put the lights on, remembered that this meant his electric chair was live, and so, just as the odd job man began to say something, he flipped the switch to off. The lights went out.

"Oooh!" exclaimed the odd job man. And then, with perspicacity, "You've switched the lights off."

"Yes," agreed Arthur. "You see—that's the job."

"Oh, yes?" The man waited for an explanation.

"Yes. You see... I would like you to... um, switch the lights *on*."

"Oh." The man said this with a wealth of meaning, but Arthur didn't have a clue what it meant.

"Do you think you could do that?" Arthur asked.

"What—switch the lights on?"

"Yes."

Without taking his eyes off Arthur, the odd job man reached out with his left hand, found the switch, and flicked the lights on.

"All, yes, very good," Arthur told him. "But... er, not now. Later on." And he switched the lights off again.

"Oh!" said the man, with even more incomprehensible meaning.

Arthur thought he should make a positive gesture at this point. "Now I'll give you the money in advance. Shall we say five... er... a tenner?" And he fumbled a ten-pound note out of his wallet and gave it to the odd job man.

The man looked at it. "To switch the lights on?"

"That's right."

The odd job man switched the lights on. He looked at Arthur expectantly. Arthur sighed and switched them off again.

"Not yet. Would you mind waiting till I sit down?"

The odd job man fought a silent battle with himself and won. "Just... er...."

"Yes," said Arthur, allowing impatience to enter his voice.

"Just... let me get this.... You're going to sit over there in that chair, and I'm going...." As he spoke, the odd job man seemed to see the wires for the first time. Arthur could practically see it all clicking through his brain. "... And you... and I... er... oh, no.... You don't..." and he came to the final inevitable conclusion: "You could get killed!"

"Yes," said Arthur firmly. "I could." And he gave the man a long hard look.

The odd job man shifted uneasily from one foot to the other. His little bird eyes flashed around the room. Once again the circuits and relays and transistors of his brain hummed and clicked. And eventually out chattered the next inescapable conclusion.

"You *want* to get killed."

"Yes." It was a relief to tell someone. Even him.

"And I'm to do it?"

"Please."

"Oh, no. No, mate, no!"

Arthur felt it was just his luck to choose a sentimentalist as an executioner.

"You'd be helping me out in a big way," he said persuasively. "I know."

"So you won't do it?"

"Not for ten quid I won't."

Arthur's heart leaped. He hadn't chosen a sentimentalist. He'd chosen a capitalist. "You mean, it's the money?"

"Bloody right it is. Do you know what they'd charge in the East End for this? Five hundred oncers!"

Arthur's heart sank again. "But I haven't got five hundred... oncers."

The odd job man gave Arthur the look that car salesmen give you when you say you can't afford the new model. Sheer disbelief. Then he looked round the room in a pointed way. "Oh, yeah?" he commented.

"I mean on me," Arthur explained. "I'll give you a cheque."

"What?" The odd job man was both incredulous and derisive. "For this sort of job? Naw, mate!"

What does he think I'd do afterwards? Arthur asked himself. Cancel it? Ring up the bank from heaven.

The odd job man began a slow stroll around the room. He had the air of a dealer in an auction room. Expertly he examined the bottoms of vases, the signatures on paintings, the imprints on old books. Arthur winced when he opened the drawers of the "Queen Anne" desk and sneered at the plywood. Still, he seemed relatively optimistic.

"You must have something in here worth five hundred," he suggested.

"How about an answering machine?"

"Eh?"

"Very handy in your sort of business," Arthur urged.

"Yeah?" The man showed slight interest. "What's it do?"

Arthur began to explain. "Well, when you're out doing a job, somewhere, and someone phones you to do…."

The odd job man cut him short. "Nobody ever phones."

"How do you know, if you're out?"

"I don't have a phone."

Arthur wanted to stuff the man's beret down his throat. Instead, he adopted the bright smile and winning ways of an electrical goods salesman.

"How about a colour telly?" he suggested.

"Mmmmm." Luke-warm.

"And with it," Arthur continued flashily, feeling that he'd missed his vocation, "You can have this!"

"This" was his TV video game. Deftly, Arthur plugged the thing in and switched on. The familiar little white blob began sailing across the screen.

"Look," he enthused. "You can play football, tennis, squash…"

One look at the odd job man's face told him he'd made a sale. The man was flushed, grinning, his eyes brighter than ever.

"Oh," he exclaimed, "that's more like it! Let's have a go."

"There isn't time," Arthur began reluctantly. "Couldn't you try it afterwards…?"

But that was no good. The odd job man wanted to try it right away. Reluctantly Arthur showed him the controls.

"See… move that, and it stops the ball and sends it back. Now, try yours…."

After three minutes of practice it became clear to Arthur that the odd job man had the dexterity, the subtlety and the insight of a rhinoceros. Fist clenched and furious, the little man operated his control this way and that, hopelessly uncoordinated, ludicrously inaccurate, pathetically slow. Point after point he lost. Each time the little blob of light floated towards him, he missed it.

"Let me help you!" Arthur was desperate. He put his hand over the odd job man's and felt it jerking and pulsating with tension.

Another miss. And another. And then, by some happy accident, the odd job man succeeded in returning a ball. Carefully Arthur missed it. The little man had scored a goal.

With a yell of triumph, he leaped to his feet. "I did it! Did you see that? I scored!" And he jumped, reaching for the ceiling and punching the air with his little fist.

"Very good," said Arthur. "Very well done. You'll take it, then?"

"Oh…." The odd job man clearly wanted another go. But he nodded.

"I'll give you a hand to take it downstairs," Arthur said helpfully.

The odd job man considered. "I'll have to go and get my motorbike and sidecar first… or, tell you what, I could kill you first… but then it would be murder."

"What?" Arthur shuddered at the word.

"Trying to get this downstairs on my own," the man explained. He clicked his fingers. "Got it. I'll bring a trolley. No need for you to worry."

"No," Arthur agreed, philosophically. No need

for him to worry about anything.

"If you give me the keys to this place I can come back when you're… deceased."

"Of course." Arthur fetched his spare set of keys from the desk and gave them to the odd job man.

"Ta." The man was now business-like and efficient. "Well, let's get on with the execution."

Arthur didn't like that word either. "Suicide," he corrected. He turned, looked at his electric chair, walked over to it. Then he came back and held out his hand to the odd job man.

"Well, good-bye then," he said. "And I forgive you."

The odd job man shook hands. "What for?" he asked. "For that which you are about to do."

"Oh, yes. I get you. Very nice knowing you, and I hope we meet again."

Arthur didn't wish to die with a lie on his lips, but he couldn't avoid this one. "Yes," he agreed.

With dignity, and again with a sense of *déjà vu,* he walked to the chair. He was in the act of sitting down when the odd job man spoke.

"Oh… er…."

Arthur froze in an "S" position. "What?"

"It's just that if it burns you up a little, you know, do you want me to finish you off?"

Arthur stared at him. "Burns me up a little?"

"Yeah, you see…." As he spoke the odd job man switched on the light.

Arthur leaped away from the chair in fright. "Will you be careful with that thing!" he snapped.

"You see," the odd job man began again, "you could just get badly hurt, with this."

Arthur was horrified. "But I want to go fast. Not… slowly, in agony."

"You picked the wrong way, mate. Could be real bad, that."

Arthur didn't understand. "But in America… the electric chair?"

The odd job man was clearly an expert on the American electric chair. "That don't look like this. They don't plug it into a light socket. Whole town's electricity supply goes in that. Woomft! Straight out. What a sight!"

None of this was any help to Arthur. He needed to be fried, not singed. Angrily he tore away the wires from the light fitting and turned on the odd job man.

"Well—what do you suggest?"

The odd job man took his time in considering the question. He strolled to and fro and sucked his teeth. Arthur waited. Then, perhaps predictably, the man picked up the Samurai sword.

"Aha!" he exclaimed.

"I thought about that," Arthur told him, "but you can't…."

As he spoke, the odd job man put his hand on the sword handle and drew it smoothly from the sheath.

It transpired that he was also an expert on the means of death in Japan.

"This is what the Japs use for suicide. They call it Hari Krishna. Right messy old business, all your intestines, bowels, liver, stomach—*and* its contents… everywhere… makes a terrible mess of the carpet." He pointed floorwards. "Persian, is it?"

"No idea." Frankly, Arthur was more concerned about the terrible mess the sword would make on him.

"You see," said the odd job man, in true pub bore style, "the great thing about dying a natural death is, you never know when it's going to happen."

"But I don't want to hang around for that!"

Arthur exclaimed. "It could take twenty or thirty years."

"Exactly." Nothing would deter the odd job man from his tedious route to a conclusion. "Now, your suicide… well, you know when that's going to happen, because it's you that's doing it."

"I realize that."

"Now you're not too keen on knowing, are you?"

A sigh. "No."

"Well, then, why don't you leave the whole arrangement in *my* hands?"

Now wait a moment, the man had something there. He really had something there! He also, Arthur noted, had the Samurai sword, and Arthur cautiously took it from him, and put it out of the way on the floor. Then he said: "You mean, you'll just do it?"

"Yeah. When you're not expecting it."

"That sounds much better." Arthur felt as if he was emerging from the end of a long dark tunnel. "It'll just happen."

"Yeah."

Arthur made up his mind. "Well… let's do that then. Thank you very much."

"Not at all."

They shook hands. Their eyes met. They were agreed. Arthur's fate was decided. It was settled.

The odd job man turned to go—and then whirled back and grabbed Arthur round the throat.

Arthur nearly died of shock.

Desperately he grabbed for the man's wrists, and held them. The muscles felt like iron. He couldn't shift the grip. Instinctively he reached out and grabbed the odd job man by the throat. It wasn't difficult, because his arms were much longer. Pop-eyed, they stared across at each other, each man squeezing the spark of life out of his opponent. Then gradually Arthur's size and reach began to tell.

Squeezing steadily, he advanced on the odd job man, forcing him to step backwards. He felt the man's fingers on his throat begin to weaken, saw the flash of panic in the eyes, and forced him back yet another step.

This time the odd job man trod on the Samurai sword. His heel slipped on the blade, and he fell' sideways. Off balance, Arthur fell after him.

Together they crashed to the carpet. The shock of the fall loosened Arthur's grip, and suddenly the odd job man was winning again. He was kneeling on Arthur's chest, digging his thumbs painfully into his larynx, squeezing.

Arthur stared up at his face. It wore a look of intense concentration.

"Don't fight it!" The odd job man yelled. "Don't fight it!"

Arthur couldn't reply. He could hardly breathe. He thrashed about with his legs, and heard the vague crash of breaking pottery. He thrashed harder. More crashes. He wondered if he'd broken the stereo amplifier. It didn't really matter; he had promised himself a new one....

But now Arthur was tiring. Sensing victory, the odd job man tightened his hold on Arthur's throat, and eased himself further up Arthur's chest. He was going for the kill.

Then Arthur had a good idea. He brought his right knee up sharply. It connected briskly with the odd job man's rear, and projected him in a low arc over Arthur's head to land face first on the carpet.

In a flash Arthur was on him, pulled him over onto his back, sat on his chest, and... rested. He was far too heavy. The odd job man was helpless.

Panting, gasping, Arthur choked out the obvious question: "What are you doing?"

The odd job man was both defensive and accusing as he produced the obvious answer: "I'm trying to kill you."

"I realize that," Arthur told him with exasperation. "But I told you that I didn't want to know when it was going to happen."

"But I didn't tell you, did I?" The man's voice rang with injured innocence.

"No, but I saw you coming at me."

"Well, look, if you get off me and go and stand facing the window," the odd job man suggested, "I'll sneak up on you and do it."

Arthur wondered how any man could be so stupid. "But I'll *know* that you'll be sneaking up on me, won't I?"

"I'll be very quiet."

Arthur couldn't help himself. In the face of such blind crass inexplicable dumbness, he lost his grip. Or to be more accurate, he found his grip—a grip on the odd job man's ears—and without really meaning to, he began banking the man's head up and down on the carpet.

And as he banged, he chanted rhythmically: "Look-I-don't-think-I'm-getting-through-to-you!"

He gave him three more bangs for luck, then stopped. And was suddenly very ashamed of himself.

Muttering apologies, he helped the odd job man to his feet, and then to a seat on the sofa. He looked shattered, and Arthur felt terrible. Quickly he went to the drinks cabinet and poured two large scotches. The odd job man accepted his with a painful nod, and together they sat on the sofa and sipped. In some curious way, Arthur felt, the incident had drawn them closer together. They felt like old friends.

The odd job man clearly felt the same, because he turned to Arthur, and put his hand gently on his shoulder.

Arthur jumped so violently, his drink flared into the air and splashed across the stereo.

"You're very jumpy," the odd job man commented.

"Well, you *did* just try to strangle me."

"Well, you just told me to do it."

They'd reached an impasse again. Arthur decided to forget what had just happened, and try again.

"Look, do it tomorrow, when I'm more prepared. Right?"

"That's fine by me." The odd job man drained his glass.

"And, er...." Arthur decided to make things quite clear. "Make it sudden. I don't want a lingering death. And do make sure I am dead. I don't want to wake up in a couple of days, badly... er "

"Mutilated?"

"Quite."

The odd job man smiled. He was clearly an expert on death in general. "Don't worry yourself, mate. I used to work in a hospital. I know when someone's dead all right."

He put out his hand, and Arthur nearly took it. Just in time he remembered, and raised his hand palm outwards and backed off.

A thought struck the odd job man. "'ere, why not go for a nice little walk in the park. Lots of places for me to hide."

"Mmm." Arthur considered. "All right. The park. I'll keep wandering around until... I don't. Good. Well, till tomorrow."

"Yes. Tomorrow."

"And *not* before," Arthur emphasized.

"And not before," the odd job man agreed.

"And," Arthur made this as plain as was humanly possible, "no matter what I say or do, you *will* go through with it. Eh?"

The odd job man smiled, and gave a quirky little nod and a wink. "It'll be a pleasure," he said.

Six

Three people nearly killed Arthur before he got to the park the next morning.

They were a bus driver and two ordinary private motorists. At least, they appeared to be ordinary private motorists. But the truth was, one was a so-called chauffeur at an East European embassy, who was returning after an all-night tryst with a lubricious typist from Treasury Records, and the other was a man who believed that, a year previously, he had been picked up and examined by alien beings from a flying saucer. The bus driver was an ordinary bus driver.

All three became aware of Arthur rather suddenly, as they motored down the Euston Road. One moment the road was its normal lethal race-track self. The next, there was this lunatic pedestrian, swanning blithely across in the face of the oncoming death. All three drivers applied their brakes with catatonic intensity and shut their eyes. All three came to rest in a cacophony of scraping brake linings, burning tyres and thumping hearts. Arthur survived—indeed, he was barely aware that anything had happened—and he gained the pavement and walked on up a side road to Regent's Park, therein to meet his fate.

The two car drivers wiped their mouths with the back of their hands, then drove on to their own private and peculiar destinies. The bus driver wondered aloud why everything happened to him.

In the park, Arthur wondered when something was going to happen to him. He had wandered about now for half an hour. It was surprising how the business of waiting for death could so quickly become boring.

At first it had been exciting and uplifting—almost an ethereal experience. All his senses seemed heightened. He could hear the clip of every nail in his shoes as he walked the tarmac paths. The flowers had never smelled so piercingly beautiful. The bird song was a carefully orchestrated symphony, and he could follow every single theme without effort. The trees in the distance waved their leaves at him, and he could see every leaf, every bud, every twig. The world was a beautiful place, and he was leaving it. He stifled a sentimental sob, and his eyes misted, and the beautiful world blurred. Arthur experienced the ecstasy of knowing that his final moment had come.

But when the final moment had stretched out to thirty minutes or more, the ecstasy wore thin. The world looked a little less beautiful. He began to notice litter and dog-turds.

Where was the odd job man?

The park wasn't empty. A gardener was digging away in a patch of bushes. Across one of the football pitches an old woman exercised her dog. She was shrieking "Fetch!" at it, and awkwardly throwing a stick, while the dog watched in puzzled silence. Two boys idly kicked a football between them. A British Rail night worker sat on a bench, waiting for ten o'clock when his wife would have gone off to work, and it would be safe for him to go home. An old man hobbled painfully along the grass, clutching a paper bag full of scraps and pursuing a pigeon, which was already so full of buckshee bread it couldn't fly. Arthur mentally told the old chap to slow down. At that moment he looked nearer the grave than Arthur himself.

If Arthur was near the grave at all. Which he had

begun to doubt.

It was perfectly feasible, he knew, that the odd job man had chickened out. But he doubted it. He remembered the look of sheer bliss which had crossed that perky little face when he had finally mastered the video game. A man whose life clearly progressed from one failure to another would not deliberately cut himself off from a facet of life in which he had known success—even the fleeting success of scoring a goal in a TV football game. Arthur was sure that the little man would fulfil his side of the bargain.

But in that case, where the hell was he? Arthur turned a full 360° circle, searching the horizon. He could see nothing and nobody unusual.

Perhaps he was waiting in the wrong place. He was in the centre of the soccer pitch area, walking to and fro and affecting a casual nonchalance in the way he kicked at the daisies. Perhaps he was too exposed.

Deliberately he made for a wooded area. And as the trees and bushes closed around him, he was sure he'd made the right decision. The shadows and the underfoot rustling seemed the very stuff of murder. He was wondering whether to keep walking, or just wait, when he heard... a noise!

He wasn't sure what it was. But it was close. He was sure, he was quite sure that the odd job man had found him. He tensed himself, wrapped his bent arms up against his chest, dug his fingernails into his palms. Nothing happened.

And then he heard the noise again. This time, because he was still and silent, he was able to pinpoint where it came from. It was just behind a tall purply bush.

Arthur hesitated, then walked up to the bush and cleared his throat, to announce his presence. There was no response.

He called out, quietly but intently: "Hello! I'm here!"

Still nothing. Finally he poked his head around the bush.

A tall thin man, with a straggly beard, was urinating on the other side.

Arthur gave him a weak smile and headed for the open park again.

By now he was disconsolate, annoyed, and very puzzled. He stopped on a small bridge over the lake, and gazed at the ducks. There could be innumerable reasons why nothing had happened. Like… like… well, maybe the odd job man had a bad memory for faces. Perhaps he was poised, ready to kill him right now, at that instant, but didn't dare in case he killed the wrong man.

Arthur indulged in a ruse. He clicked his fingers at the ducks, calling to them.,

"Here ducks… here ducks…" and then he raised his voice to a clear, distinct tone. "I'm *here*… ducks… here I am… Come to Arthur… *Arthur Harris*…."

Two housewives coming down the path by the lake stopped and looked at Arthur. Then they looked at each other. Then they hurried on. Arthur felt rather foolish.

He felt even more foolish a moment later, when he remembered that at no time during the conversation the day before had he told the odd job man his name. Angrily, he straightened up and decided to go home. He strode off down the path, alongside a line of trees, angrily grumbling about himself to himself:

"Bloody fool you are, he doesn't know who Arthur Harris is, doesn't know Arthur Harris from—"

CLUNK!

The odd job man accomplished the blow with style. He felt pleased with himself. He simply waited behind the birch, or whatever tree it was, he didn't know, and when Arthur came by he raised his shovel and belted him one. Arthur fell like the very drunk. A quick glance to each side, then a hand under each arm, and the odd job man dragged him into a small clump of trees.

It had been a neat operation, and worth taking time over. He'd been there since early morning. He'd been the gardener, digging away in the bushes. He'd dug a good hole. Two feet wide, six feet long, four feet deep. A suitable shape, he thought.

By the side of the hole stood another item essential for his plan—a big litter bin trolley. It was, unfortunately, dark green in colour. The odd job man felt that, for the purpose to which it would be put, it should be black.

He finished dragging Arthur out of sight, into the trees, then walked back out to the path and looked. No, the body couldn't be seen. Fine. He turned and went back to get the trolley. Albert Johnstone was the old man intent on force-feeding the pigeon. He was a very old man. He was what the welfare visitor called a "good age." He often wondered what was good about it.

The failings of age vary. The effects can be surprising. Albert, for instance, developed a super-charged intensity of purpose. This had been no part of his make-up as a young man. Then he'd been so vacillating, he'd once been in danger of a charge of bigamy. He just hadn't bothered to see his divorce through.

But now, in his eighties, Albert made up for his early inconsistency. Now, as people knew to their cost, when Albert Johnstone was set on a course, he was not to be denied.

If he wanted to tell someone a story over a pint, then he would continue with that story until the end, even if by then the original listener was finishing his second game of darts on the other side of the bar.

Similarly, if he wanted to feed scraps from yesterday's indigestible meal-on-wheel to a pigeon, then he would feed that pigeon, though lake, wood and flower bed, to say nothing of the sated bird, conspired to oppose him.

Which was why he tottered after the damn thing as it went up the path, across the grass, through the shrubs, into the trees, out onto the grass again, and on and on until the breath rasped in his throat and his heart shook in his chest and all he could think of was to shove the last of the muck in his paper bag down the throat of that bird, and so it was with a last staggering effort of will that he charged after the thing through a final group of shrubs, until he and the bird came to the odd job man's hole, over which the pigeon hopped and into which he fell. And didn't move.

Two minutes later the odd job man arrived at the hole in a big rush. Leather coat swirling, he grabbed the handles of the litter bin trolley, and was trying for a real grand prix getaway in the direction of Arthur's body when he saw a foot sticking out of the hole.

At first he thought it must be a joke, and he looked around to see who was laughing at him. But there was no one.

He went to the edge of the hole and looked in. Annoyance set in. He clicked his tongue, then climbed into the pit and shook the body.

"Oi! Come on! Get out! It's not yours."

He shook more violently. The body dangled limply, the old head hanging back. The odd job man lowered the body down onto the earth. His expertise came into play. He checked the eyes, and they gleamed whitely. He listened for the heart, felt for the pulse, but registered neither. He sat back on his knees and sighed.

Then he stood up in the hole and looked around. No one was watching. Quickly he straightened the body in the hole, then climbed out. He grabbed the trolley, and began to push it back to where he'd left Arthur.

Arthur thought he must be dead and was vaguely disappointed with death. It seemed just as painful as being alive. No, more so.

Then he opened his eyes, and found himself nose down in the dirt staring at the wrapper of a Cadbury's Fruit and Nut bar. This could only mean that, for the second time in two days, he'd been knocked unconscious.

Across the wrapper crawled an insect of repulsive appearance. Arthur jerked his head back instinctively, and the shock waves hammered against the back of his head. He wondered if his skull was fractured. He wondered how he'd know if it was. He lay still again and waited to feel better.

Then he remembered the odd job man. Clearly the man had hit him. But not killed him. Why not? The thought occurred to Arthur that perhaps the death-dealing little gnome was at that moment standing sadistically above him, implement in hand, waiting only for Arthur to realize his predicament before administering a last vicious *coup de grace.*

He raised his head and looked around. He was in a clump of trees. Vaguely he could see the more open expanse of the park beyond. He could see no one. Then he heard a voice. It was distant, and female, and it seemed to be shrieking some mortal agony of the spirit.

Arthur struggled to ignore the pain in his head. It seemed to him vital that he concentrated until he could make out what the voice was saying. He tried his best, and soon the words did indeed become distinct.

The unknown girl was screaming: "I tell you, Rodney, the sodding ball was out!"

Arthur lumbered to his feet. His eyes blurred, his legs wobbled. Mumbling to himself, he stumbled through the trees and away.

The odd job man manoeuvred his trolley up and along the paths. He imagined it might be easier to wrestle a wild steer in a rodeo.

The problem was, he was in a hurry, and the trolley was not designed for rapid movement. It was designed to be trundled at a respectable pace from litter bin to litter bin, in the hands of elderly, calm and staid litter bin trolley operators.

It objected to being jerked and shoved in haste. It resented being charged over verges, pulled sideways, hauled around sharp corners, lugged over tree roots, and generally treated with a lack of regard and respect. So it fought back, swinging wildly out of control at every opportunity, dropping gleefully into deep ruts and potholes, locking its wheels, jarring its handles, and making life for the odd job man as difficult as possible. But he fought back, and eventually persuaded the thing to enter the group of trees where Arthur's body lay.

Only the body wasn't there any longer. The odd job man abandoned the trolley and rushed about among the trees in a panic. At first he thought he'd mistaken the place and rapidly widened the area of search. When this was no more successful, he came back to his starting place, and at once he found his shovel. He had to accept that Arthur had gone.

Leaving the trolley behind, he walked slowly back to his hole in the ground, dragging the shovel behind him. The hole at least was undisturbed from when he last looked at it. The old man sill lay in it. The odd job man sighed, shrugged, and filled it in.

Arthur found himself staggering the wrong way down Albany Street. Automatically he turned and began to make his way towards home. He felt sick and tired, but most of all, disappointed. He still wasn't dead. All the build-up without the final climax. Mortus Interruptus.

It would still come, of course. At any time. Perhaps even now the odd job man was stalking up behind him, taking cover behind parking meters, loading a high velocity rifle, zeroing in on the back of Arthur's neck. All well and good. Let it come. Meanwhile he was going home for a drink. Moodily he entered the flats and took the lift to his floor. He unlocked the door, mooched through the hall, into the sitting room—and let out a startled cry. Someone was already there, waiting for him.

Seven

It was Fiona.

Arthur's shout of alarm turned into a yelp of joy, which, just as rapidly, he muffled.

"Arthur," said Fiona, gazing at him. To Arthur she seemed sad and humble. She looked as if she had come to make it up. But he didn't dare allow himself to believe it. Instead he made his own face dull and formal, his voice cool and uninvolved.

"Forgotten something, have you?"

"Yes, I'd... forgotten that I love you."

The world once more swam before Arthur's eyes. "What?" he asked stupidly.

"Will you forgive me? I've been so stupid, letting little things annoy me. And the thought of your dying really depressed me."

Just as he couldn't believe it when she'd told him she didn't love him, now Arthur couldn't believe she was telling him she did. But only for another moment. Then he did believe it. He felt his face breaking into a smile, and the muscles felt stiff and creaky with disuse. He stood there, all loose and happy, and he grinned at her.

"Oh, Arthur!" Fiona wailed, and began to come apart emotionally. Tears flowing, arms flailing, she crossed the space between them and fell into his arms.

Arthur held her. He felt like Tarzan. He felt like Rudolph Valentino. He felt like... yes, he felt like Rod Stewart! He'd won his girl back again. His rival was beaten. She was his! Victory was his! The victory of the young stallion!

Fiona's voice was muffled by tears and his coat

front. "I'm sorry. I was so worried about you. I'm glad you didn't do anything silly."

Hot relief flooded through Arthur's body as he registered what she'd said.

"So am I!" he breathed.

It was uncanny how the whole prospect of his future had changed in one single instant. Before it had been the cold finality of death which he faced. Now it was endless days of life and happiness with the woman he loved. He breathed deeply. It was true, life *was* sweet. He hugged Fiona to him and closed his eyes, promising himself that he would never tell her how close he'd come to ending it all, how narrowly he'd escaped death. He'd never mention the scenes in the flat the day before, or in the park that morning. It would remain a secret known only to him, and, of course, the odd job man.

The odd job man....

A nameless panic clutched at Arthur's heart.

He opened his eyes. Over Fiona's shoulder he could see through the balcony window. Over to the right was another block of flats, also with balconies. And on the balcony level with Arthur was a figure. Holding something long and thin....

... a high velocity rifle!

Arthur's stomach turned a somersault. For a second he stared in desperate panic. Then, like some blackbelt judoka, he swept his right leg violently against Fiona.

"Ooooooh!"

Fiona found herself falling sideways, out of control, Arthur coming down on top of her. By a stroke of luck, she fell on the sofa. Arthur landed a fifth of a second later.

"Ooof!"

Arthur found his face buried in Fiona's bosom, his nose up against a rather hard button. His right knee was between hers, and her right knee had come to within an inch of dealing him a very nasty one indeed. To steady herself Fiona had grabbed his hair, and that did hurt. Inevitably, with hardly a pause, they rolled entwined from the sofa, and fell another foot to the carpet.

"Aaaah!"

This time she fell on him. And enjoyed it, too, he could tell that by the way she moved her hips against him and ducked her face into his neck. Arthur didn't have time to explain. He wondered if the sofa would shield them from the gunman's fire. He couldn't take the risk. He put one hand on Fiona's bottom, the other round her shoulders, and lifted her over and down, rolling his body on top of hers. Now she'd be safe.

"Ooooooooooh!"

This time Fiona's sigh was one of anticipation. Clearly she expected and welcomed a reunion scene of mutual rape. Arthur felt she was going to be disappointed. He felt it might be difficult to maintain a hearty rut while momentarily expecting a bullet in the bum. And anyway, his right arm was trapped beneath her and beginning to go to sleep.

"Oh, Arthur!"

She put an arm round his neck, and drew him even closer. Arthur covered up like mad, by kissing her face and neck like an over-emotional teenager. Fiona seemed to like it. Desperately he wondered what to do next. Then he began gradually to slow his rate of kissing, and Fiona responded by raising a hand and stroking his face with more love than lust.

"Oh, Arthur," she breathed, "you really do forgive me?"

Good grief, thought Arthur, of course I forgive you, I just saved your life. "Oh, yes," he told her, his fearful breathless voice adding emphasis to his words, "Yes… I do."

He gave her a few more kisses and hugs. He thought how stupid they must look, rolling around on the carpet. After all, Fiona was no teenager, while he was mid… no, he wasn't middle-aged. Thirty-seven is not middle-aged. Middle-aged is forty or more. All the same….

"I'm so happy," Fiona breathed.

She was happy. At any moment a dum-dum slug could shatter its way through the window, and plough with that awful tumbling effect through his flesh, through hers, ripping into muscle and tendon, splintering bone, decimating internal organs and scattering them in bloody clumps throughout the flat, and she was happy. Ha! It would take more than a box of Kleenex to clean up the mess if it happened.

But it hadn't happened. Not yet. Maybe there was a chance.

Arthur eased his body off Fiona's, so that he lay on the carpet between her and the window. She looked in his eyes, and smiled warmly. Arthur managed a grimace.

"Let's get out of here," he suggested.

"What?" If Fiona had anticipated a move in any direction, it was definitely towards the bedroom. She didn't understand.

"To… celebrate!" Arthur told her. Good thinking.

She smiled. "Fine." Arthur could read her mind like a book. How mature, she was thinking. How thoughtful. Not a quick wham-bam in bed, but a true loving reconciliation, celebrated with good food and wine, intimate conversation, and then finally, as a climax to the hours of warm happy togetherness, back home for a real wham-bam-wham-bam-wham-bam....

Arthur felt like an unpleasant little tick.

"We'll have lunch at the San Carlo."

Fiona's eyes lit up. The San Carlo was really going it. "Oh, yes," she said.

And then Arthur nearly died. He'd relaxed his hold on her, and before he knew what she was doing, she'd said: "I'll just smarten myself up a bit," and then she had *got up*.

He made a wild desperate lunge after her, jerking his arm round and sending a shooting pain the length of his back, but missed. Fiona, unconcerned and humming happily, walked with agonizing slowness towards the hall door. From a twisted crouch on the carpet, Arthur watched her go and waited for the bullet. It didn't come. She walked into the hall and disappeared towards the bedroom.

Arthur was so relieved he nearly wet himself.

After a pause, to make sure she didn't come back, Arthur crawled across the carpet like a snake, until he reached the wall by the window. Then he eased himself up against it, until he was standing. With infinite patience, he peeped very carefully round, until he could just see the sniper's balcony.

Only it wasn't a sniper with a rifle. It was a woman with a broom.

Arthur's knees shook. Okay, so it hadn't been him that time. But he was out there somewhere. The odd job man was on the warpath and there was no way to stop him.

Shivering, Arthur seemed to hear once again the fateful conversation:

"Why don't you leave the whole arrangement in my hands?"

"You mean you'll just do it?"

"Yeah. When you're not expecting it."

"That sounds much better. It'll just happen."

"Yeah."

"Well, let's do that then. Thank you very much."

Thank you very much… he must have been bloody mad! How could he stop him? Who was he. *Where* was he? He could be waiting around any corner. Gun, axe, knife, rope… there was a million ways the man could kill him. Arthur took a deep breath. Okay then, one way or another, he'd have to fight back.

In a half-crouch, still wary of the view through the window, Arthur skittered across the sitting room and into the hall. Fiona was making "getting ready" noises in the bedroom. He whipped open the door of the hall cupboard, and dived into a pile of old clothes that had been pushed into a corner to wait for a rag-and-bone man who never came. He found what he needed quickly—the luck of the desperate, he told himself. It was his old duffle coat. It testified to a well mis-spent youth, bearing the rips and stains of drunken evenings up the Earls Court Road and elsewhere. Last time Arthur had worn it had been for redecorating the bathroom, so streaks of primrose yellow added to the general effect. In a pocket he found the crowning glory—a tatty old woolly hat that had once been de rigeur for traditional jazz clubs. It still smelled faintly of cheap beer and Gauloises. Arthur pulled on hat and coat and looked at himself in the hall mirror. He looked like an antiquated beatnik. And he felt a lot better.

Fiona, wearing a new flaming red crêpe dress and a felt hat, and looking the way you need to look when you have lunch at the San Carlo, came out of the bedroom, saw Arthur, and stopped dead.

Arthur gave her a weak smile. "Urn…" he began,

"felt like a bit of a change."

Fiona's smile was equally doubtful. "Oh," she said.

"You know," Arthur extemporized, "try to recapture the old magic."

"Oh!" This time she was pleased. She clearly thought that Arthur was making a sincere if rather absurd attempt to re-vitalize their marriage, to make up for any neglect, any routine that had crept into their lives and driven her out so abruptly two days before. How sweet of him!

Once again, Arthur felt like an unpleasant little tick.

Getting into the lift was awkward. Arthur let Fiona leave the flat first. After all, if the odd job man had got that close, he wouldn't make a mistake and kill her. So Arthur hid behind the door, waiting while Fiona pushed the lift button.

"Is there anybody on the landing?" he called quietly.

"No—why?" Fiona looked round for him and found he wasn't there.

"Oh, just felt a bit odd in this old coat—don't want anyone laughing. Are you sure there's no one?"

"Yes!" For Fiona, the joke was wearing a little thin.

Slowly Arthur looked around the door. "Nobody near the lift?"

"Nobody! Come on."

But Arthur wasn't going to do anything so stupid as to wait around on that death-trap of a landing where the odd job man could come at him from the lift itself, or up the stairs, or through the Emergency Fire Escape Door. So he waited. The lift arrived, and the doors opened.

"Anyone in the lift?" he called.

"No!" Despite herself, Fiona had to laugh. "Come on, you don't look that bad."

In one fluid movement, Arthur whipped through the door, pulled it to behind him so it locked, then sprinted across the landing into the lift. He pulled Fiona in after him, and jammed his finger against the button for the ground floor. With agonizing deliberation, the lift doors closed. For a brief moment he was safe again.

Downstairs was a different matter. As the door opened, Arthur slipped on his *pièce de résistance*—a pair of sunglasses. Then, pulling his woolly hat firmly down over his forehead, he followed Fiona out of the lift. He was, he felt, unrecognizable.

The awful caretaker came fussing out of his cubby hole.

"Afternoon, Mrs. Harris, Mr. Harris," he said. And only then did he show any surprise, giving Arthur a long mystified stare and clearly dying to make some comment about his appearance.

Arthur stared back at him over the sunglasses, with a look compounded in equal parts of loathing, antagonism and sheer madness.

The caretaker thought better of it and kept his mouth shut.

Arthur paused just inside the entrance. Sunlight streamed down on the forecourt. Ideal weather for marksmanship. Arthur thought hard.

"Race you to the car!" he told Fiona, forcing boyish enthusiasm into his voice.

Fiona shrugged and grinned. "Okay—let's go!" And she jumped down the steps and ran off towards the car, one hand holding down her hat, her knees together and ankles flying wide in the way of a woman who rarely runs.

For Arthur it was time to disinter from a faded memory his days in a school cadet force. The objective—to reach his shiny red "N" registered Rover some fifty years away across open ground. Method—to use the… what was it? The monkey run, did they call it?—and all available natural cover. Go!

He leaped sideways to crouch behind the awful caretaker's old van, in its specially reserved premium parking space. This gave him four yards of almost total cover. Then a three-yard sprint, and a one-handed vault over the low brick wall, to the patch of perfect grass. Go! Across, over, and smack into dog-shit. Move on quick, keep that head down, Harris! The wall brought him to one of the forecourt entrances. Across this entrance, and two car spaces further along, was the Rover. It looked a long way away. Fiona was already there, looking for him. Arthur cast around desperately for something to get him across the open space.

And he found it! Walking into the entrance, returning from his daily stroll with their dog, was the man of the elderly couple upstairs. Mr. Kemp.

Arthur shot out of cover, and ran up to Kemp. He stopped bang in front of him, about two inches away. Mr. Kemp nearly had a heart attack.

"Hello Mr. Kemp what a nice day for taking the little doggie for a walk then that's a good idea, just the thing for…."

Keeping up this continuous flow of babble, Arthur positioned himself so that he remained between Mr. Kemp and the flats. More important, Mr. Kemp remained between him and a possible sniper's field of fire. He put his hands on Mr. Kemp's shoulders, and, ignoring the old boy's look of amazement, shuffled him sideways across the entrance, and half the distance again towards the Rover.

"Yes I was just saying to my wife what a wonderful day to go for a walk and take a dog and…."

Arthur abandoned Mr. Kemp in mid-babble. He sprinted the last five yards in nought seconds, and finished panting, in a crouch, by the Rover.

Mr. Kemp looked after him, baffled. Fiona looked down at him, ditto.

"Well done," Arthur told her. "You won." He found his keys and opened the passenger door for her.

Fiona got in slowly, still very puzzled. "I thought it was a hundred yard dash. Not a steeple-chase," she said acidly.

Arthur hurried round the back of the car. Then he paused. A thought struck him. He carefully inserted the key in the boot handle lock, then twisted it quickly, and jerked the boot open.

It was empty.

Breathing deeply, Arthur scooted round to the driver's door, and got in.

"Why did you look in the boot?" Fiona asked, reasonably.

"Nothing…." Arthur hesitated. "Just checking we've got a spare wheel."

"But we're only going about two miles."

"And… two miles back!" Arthur was pleased with his answer. He put the key in the ignition, and was about to turn it, when another thought struck him. He sat still for a moment.

"Now what?" Fiona asked.

He turned to her and gave her a generous smile. "You drive darling."

"All right—but you hate my driving." Fiona didn't stay to argue. This was a rare treat. She opened the passenger door and ran round the car. Arthur eased himself with care over the gear lever and hand brake, and settled in the passenger seat. Indeed, he settled as far down as he could, until he was only just able to see over the dashboard. Fiona took the wheel, started up, and shot, with a certain nervous quickness, out of the forecourt and into the road.

Neither she nor Arthur saw the odd job man. He was lying in the forecourt where the car had stood. He had his hands full of spanners and clipper, and his face was streaked with oil.

He jumped up and looked around him. Then he grabbed the last of his tools, and sprinted through the entrance and around the corner to his motorcycle combination.

He threw the tools in the sidecar, jammed a helmet on his head, and kicked the machine into life. Far down the road he could still pick out the shiny red of Arthur's Rover. Fiona's choice of parking space outside the San Carlo—a plainly visible double yellow line—would normally have been the occasion for some sharp and witty observations on the female driver as a modern phenomenon. But Arthur was so busy not being shot or otherwise extinguished, he didn't even notice.

The restaurant was on Fiona's side of the car. So Arthur waited until she got out, then dived shallowly across the driver's seat, and tumbled out on the pavement on his hands and knees. Fiona, who seemed to have made up her mind not to comment on Arthur's eccentricities any further, waited while he scampered out of the way, then closed and locked the car door. By the time she looked around, Arthur was sheltering in the restaurant doorway. She joined him, and together they went inside.

The San Carlo combines the best of Italian

cooking with the best of Italian courtesy. The subtle spicy smell which immediately assaulted Arthur's nose made him suddenly aware how hungry he was. He wondered when he'd last eaten. He couldn't remember.

Then suddenly there was trouble. A small dark waiter was coming towards him, an intent look of purpose on his yellowy face. Arthur backed away, until he came up against a large potted plant. The waiter held out his arms. Arthur poised to hit him. The he saw that another waiter had approached Fiona in a similar manner, and she had given him her coat.

Fiona noticed his hesitation.

"Give him your coat, Arthur love," she said, as if Arthur was a child visiting a restaurant for the first time.

Arthur did as he was told. The waiter took the duffle coat with the air of a Rolls-Royce salesman taking a Vauxhall Cresta in part exchange. He accepted the woolly hat with similar grace. And then, with a swift movement, he hid both away behind a small counter.

Then he smiled for the first time. Indeed, with the disappearance of Arthur's coat, the whole restaurant seemed to sigh with relief.

The head waiter appeared, exercised a smoother smile, and escorted Arthur and Fiona to a well-placed table. Twisting and turning his body like a bull-fighter, he eased Fiona into the seat with its back to the wall, spread a snow-white napkin on her lap, then pulled out the other chair for Arthur.

Arthur didn't like it. His back was to the door. That was no good. That was the way some dirty sidewinder got Wild Bill Hickock. Or was it Bat Masterson? Either way, he wasn't having it.

"Er… darling," he said tentatively, "would you

mind awfully if I sat there?"

Embarrassed, Fiona glanced at the head waiter. The noble Roman face twitched not a muscle. With considerable scraping of chair and table on tiled floor, Fiona and Arthur changed places. Arthur sat down. This was better. If the odd job man appeared through the door, sawn-off shotgun at the ready, then he'd have time to throw himself to the floor and crawl under the....

"What was wrong with this seat?" Fiona interrupted his fantasy.

"Um...." Arthur thought quickly. "I couldn't see you so well... the light is better...."

"Aaah!" Fiona gave him a look of melting affection. She reached across through the forest of glassware and bread-sticks, took his hand and gave it a loving squeeze.

Arthur felt like the sort of tick that even other ticks don't talk to.

There was no possibility that Arthur or Fiona would hear the odd job man when he arrived outside the restaurant, because he allowed his motorcycle combination to freewheel the last 200 yards.

He pulled in just in front of the Rover and sat still for a moment, scanning the pavements for trouble.

Then he climbed off the bike, grabbed a handful of tools, and disappeared once again under Arthur's car.

Fiona sipped her Campari-soda and smiled lovingly across at Arthur. Arthur beamed back, and raised his gin and tonic to her, and then behind his right shoulder a waiter clattered noisily out of the kitchen laden with steaming silver dishes, and Arthur spilled gin down his shirt.

"Oh, dear," he said weakly.

Fiona got to her feet. "I think I'll just pop into the, er…" and she gestured towards the Ladies. She crossed the restaurant to the appropriate door, and the head waiter bowed her through it.

Arthur got to his feet. He wasn't happy. Too many doors. He too crossed the restaurant. The head waiter bowed him towards the Gents. Arthur took no notice and walked into the kitchen.

The scene was the usual steamy organized chaos of a commercial kitchen. The chef and his helpers at first ignored Arthur. Nothing could be allowed to interrupt the frenzied sauce-pourings and escallop-fryings. But then his behaviour soon began to draw their attention, as he went from one white-hatted figure to another, staring intently into their faces. This done, he checked cupboards and cabinets, even the cold store. He looked out the back door. Dustbins. A final check established that the odd job man was not crouching in one of them. Satisfied, he walked back through a by now silent and motionless kitchen, and from there back into the restaurant.

Here he had one more check to make. The Gents was clean and modern, and empty. He trusted that repressions and complexes would prevent the odd job man from using the Ladies. Momentarily calmer and safer, Arthur made his way back to his table, and Fiona.

Inconspicuously, the head waiter floated to the kitchen door, peeped in, and raised his eyebrows at the chef in the international gesture of interrogation. The chef shrugged at him in Italian.

Two hands emerged from underneath Arthur's

car and gripped the front bumper. A heave, and the odd job man brought his body sliding out into the open.

He got to his feet. He was clearly pleased with his work. He used an old oily rag to wipe the bumper where he'd touched it. Then, whistling cheerfully, he returned to his combination, once more threw the tools in the sidecar, and roared off.

Arthur heard the vague roar of a motorbike. He remembered the odd job man talking about his motorbike and sidecar, and he shrugged.

Another waiter appeared, heading for their table. In his hand he held a bottle of wine. Four paces behind and slightly to one side, riding shotgun, came the head waiter.

With deft ceremony, the waiter presented the label. Arthur nodded—then started with alarm. The bottle was open!

"It's open!" he told the waiter.

"Yes, sir."

Didn't the stupid man realize that this immediately raised the possibility of the wine having been poisoned in advance? He looked into the waiter's eye. Five years' experience of dealing with silly English eaters peered back at him. Arthur decided to abandon explanations.

He said simply: "I want it opened here," and tapped the table.

The head waiter ignored the silly twittering of some female customer on his left, and instead covered the four yards to Arthur's table like olive oiled lightning.

Arthur told the waiter, who hadn't moved: "I want you to bring me the same wine, only open it here in front of me."

The waiter looked to the head waiter for guidance.

The head waiter gave him guidance, augmented with words that sounded rude even if you didn't know Italian.

The waiter went. The head waiter apologised. "Sorry, sir," and then, as if it explained everything, "He comes from the North of Italy."

Arthur nodded. Perhaps that did explain everything. "Oh," he said.

The head waiter enquired as to the condition of Arthur's gin and tonic. Arthur confirmed that it was as well as could be expected. The head waiter widened his query to include Madame's Campari-soda, and was similarly reassured.

The waiter returned with a new bottle of wine. The head waiter treated him to an utterly meaningless click of the fingers. The waiter treated the head waiter to an extremely meaningful look. It appeared rude even if you didn't know Italian. The head waiter glided away, while the other began again the ceremony of the wine.

Arthur waited patiently. The waiter showed him the label, and Arthur was also able to check that the seal around the cork was unbroken. Without too much trouble, the waiter pulled the cork, and poured a little of the wine into Arthur's glass. Arthur picked it up and sniffed it. Then he put it down heavily in front of the waiter.

"Sir?" the waiter queried.

"Taste it," Arthur ordered.

"Me?"

At that precise moment, the middle-aged lady from Barnes, who was describing to the head waiter her version of the zabaglione, had just finished the phrase "the perfect emulsification of wine and cream" when she realized she was talking to thin air.

The head waiter had dematerialized. He rematerialized by Arthur's table.

"How is the wine, sir?"

"Don't know," Arthur said bluntly. "He hasn't tasted it for me yet."

Fiona sighed. In a voice that betrayed both exasperation and embarrassment, she said, "I'll taste it," and reached across for the glass.

Arthur put real iron into his voice. "No! No!"

The head waiter turned to the waiter and put old-world Italian courtesy into his voice, and told him to piss off. In Italian.

He turned back to Arthur. "Permit me." He indicated the departing waiter with a nod. "His mother was Swiss," he explained. "They know nothing about wine."

Then he lifted the glass to his lips and sipped. Arthur waited.

The head waiter's face distorted in sudden agony. His hands flew up arid grasped his throat. He staggered.

Arthur watched the head waiter's sufferings, and felt pleased that he had not been making a fool of himself, and that he had avoided the danger only by taking rigorous precautions. He then felt scared, because the odd job man was demonstrating his deadly cunning and determination. He forgot to feel anything for the head waiter.

The head waiter's face cleared, and he stood up straight. He smiled. "The wine is perfect, sir," he said. And then, seeing the expression on Arthur's face, "My little joke, eh?"

Arthur could have killed him.

Police Sergeant Brunton enjoyed his work. He enjoyed taking statements from weeping women shoplifters. He enjoyed questioning road accident victims as they bled on casualty floors. Most of all, he enjoyed driving away illegally parked cars.

Arthur's car, on the double yellow lines, was like a Red Rover to a Bull.

There were several cars parked illegally outside the San Carlo. Enough for all the policemen who tumbled out of their van. But the sergeant picked out Arthur's at once.

"I'll have that one," he told Pc Robbins. "You take the mini."

Pc Robbins thought that was a very poor idea. "Oh, come on, sarge," he moaned, his thin little face wearing its usual expression of irritation. "You had that Mustang yesterday. I always get the minis or vans. All the dull stuff."

The sergeant watched as a third constable went along the line of cars, unlocking them from a huge bunch of keys. He tapped his stripes with blatant pride.

"When you've got these, laddie," he said, "you can do what you like. Until such times as you do have these, you'll do as I like."

Pc Robbins thought about the day when he would have sergeant's stripes, and promised himself he'd be an even bigger bastard than Brunton.

Sergeant Brunton squeezed himself into the Rover, and adjusted the seat. Then he started the engine, and swung the thing out and down the road with a flourish. In his mirror he saw Robbins in the mini come spurting after him.

The policeman enjoyed the ride. They drove fast. They kept the revs high, they rode the clutches, they stamped on the brakes, they really made those cars move!

Sergeant Brunton was like most men—he thought of himself as an expert driver. So it was particularly galling that, as they progressed down towards the river, he missed his gears at a traffic light.

With a wild whoop Pc Robbins shot past in the mini.

Brunton grunted. The sod! He put his foot down and steamed after Robbins.

The river approached, gleaming dully in the sunlight. Fifty yards ahead, the mini's lights gleamed red, as Robbins braked, then took a sharp left turn to head east down the embankment.

Brunton reckoned to gain on braking distance. He waited until the last second. Then he clamped on the anchors.

Nothing happened.

Brunton didn't panic. Rovers hold the road well. He could make the bend without brakes. Judging the moment carefully, he twisted the wheel to the left.

Nothing happened.

The Rover shot straight on, mounted the kerb, bumped across the paved area, glanced off a bollard, and nose-dived into the Thames.

By the time Pc Robbins had reversed back up the street to where the other policemen had stopped, the roof of the Rover was just disappearing beneath the green water.

Robbins considered diving in, and effecting a rescue. But he sincerely doubted that his life-saving abilities were sufficiently advanced.

And in any case, this meant there'd now be a vacancy for sergeant.

Eight

Arthur downed his second brandy in one, and plonked the glass back on the table. Brandy, he told himself, is good for the digestion. After all he'd eaten, it would have to be. Grilled prawns, veal in white wine, some enormous sticky chocolate cake, two square inches of Brie—once Arthur had established that there was no danger of food of drink being poisoned, he'd eaten like a schoolboy. Was it stuffing for security, he wondered? Oral gratification in time of stress? Or just a case of the condemned man eating a hearty lunch?

The sound of glass on table brought the head waiter at full skate.

He beamed at them: "Enjoy your meal, sir? madame?"

"Very much," said Fiona, anxious to please the poor man.

"Excellent," Arthur agreed.

A subtle change came over the head waiter. "No... er... complaints?"

Arthur shook his head. "No." He looked at Fiona.

"No, none." She was positive.

The head waiter glowed.

"Can we have the bill, please?" Arthur asked.

The head waiter appeared not to hear. "Not even the smallest complaint?"

"No, really."

"A tiny tiny one?"

Arthur looked at the man. What did he want? A congratulatory kiss on both cheeks? You can never tell with these Mediterranean types. Arthur gave him a very British masculine nod.

"I assure you it was excellent," he said firmly. And then, "If we could just have the...."

The head waiter cut him off with a formal bow. "Thank you, sir." He clapped his hands and a waiter rushed for their coats. Then he turned to Arthur again, and, incredibly, he winked.

Arthur had to work hard not to wink back. It wasn't a wink of sexual suggestion. Nor a wink of secret amusement. It was a wink of complicity, of shared knowledge. The kind of wink two men exchange when they've met before at a VD clinic. We two know something, it said. Nobody else knows except us. Aren't we special!

Fiona was worrying about the bill. "Perhaps we pay at the door," she suggested.

They both began to get up. The head waiter swanned around, moving chairs, moving tables, moving waiters, making the path straight. Gently, he escorted them to the door.

Arthur produced his wallet. "Look, the bill..." he began.

The head waiter put his finger to his lips and shushed him. It was as if they'd been invited guests at a formal lunch, and had volunteered to lend a hand with the washing up. Don't mention it, the gesture told them. Don't even think about it.

A waiter held out Arthur's scruffy duffle and woolly hat. The head waiter took personal charge, and eased Arthur into the sleeves with all the care and concern he normally reserved for Savile Row duffel coats. And then, as he straightened Arthur's collar, he leaned forward and whispered in his ear.

"Egon Ronay?"

Arthur struggled with the Italian accent. Egg? No, it's yellow paint from the bathroom.

"What?" he said.

"Michelin?" the head waiter suggested.

Car tyres, Arthur registered. The man was babbling. "Look," he began, "I don't...."

"The Times?"

The man was offering him a newspaper now. Arthur shook his head. "No, I...."

But now they were at the restaurant door, which the head waiter swung open with a flourish. He turned to Arthur and Fiona and carefully shook hands with them. It was the warm, firm, honest, civilized handshake of the man who is trying to impress on you how warm, firm, honest and civilized he is.

"It's been a pleasure having you," he said.

Arthur turned as he stepped out onto the pavement, and took a last look back at this extraordinary man. At the kitchen door, a small crowd of waiters and cooks had gathered. When they saw him looking, they all waved at him. In Italian.

Arthur let the door close behind him.

Gin, wine, brandy and food had conspired to dull the naked edge of his fear. He had survived the lunch. He had come safely through a public meal in an Italian restaurant—a feat which, Arthur thought with a giggle—was sufficiently hazardous even when you're not being hunted by a lethal loony.

Nonetheless, he took a careful look up and down the street. There was no sign of anything to worry about. He sighed. Perhaps the odd job man had given up. He looked again. No, wait a minute—something *was* wrong.

The wine and brandy had gone to Fiona's head, and she was idly playing hopscotch on the pavement slabs and giggling about the head waiter and getting away without paying... but that wasn't what was wrong.

What was it?

Then suddenly Arthur knew what it was.

The car had gone!

"The car's gone!" he told Fiona.

"Oh, no!"

The Rover was certainly not where Fiona had parked it. She and Arthur looked around frantically. Perhaps someone had moved it slightly. But it wasn't anywhere in sight. They ran in different directions down the pavements, to peer around corners, but it wasn't there either. They met up again outside the restaurant and looked helplessly at each other.

Then Fiona spotted help. It was in the shape of the rather plump bottom of Pc Fielding. The top half of the constable was buried in the engine of an ancient Ford Thames van. On the roof of the van stood the constable's helmet. A dead giveaway.

Pc Fielding was in a filthy mood. Trust his luck to be told to drive away a car that wouldn't start. Even that berk Robbins got a working mini. While he got this load of crap. Angrily, he wrenched at the distributer head and broke a clip.

"Shit!" he said.

"Excuse me," said Arthur, tapping him on the bottom. Pc Fielding's head shot up and hit the bonnet.

"My car's been stolen," Arthur told him.

"Call Interpol!" said Pc Fielding, rubbing his head.

"No, really. It's been stolen."

Pc Fielding took a long look at Arthur's flushed face. Then he looked at Fiona. For the first time a certain vague interest shone in his eyes, and he stood up straighter.

"Where was it parked?"

"There…." Arthur pointed dramatically to the wide empty section of roadside by the restaurant. "It was a red Rover—three thousand five hundred."

The constable began to show much greater interest. He leered happily at Fiona. Then, summoning up a facile memory for the inconsequential, he told Arthur the registration number of Arthur's car.

"But how…?"

The constable capped his performance with: "Slight dent on the nearside wing."

"Eh?" Arthur shook his head, puzzled.

Fiona went a medium shade of plum. "Oh… I did that last Tuesday afternoon…. I was going to tell you…."

"Ah." Arthur conceded. "That's my car."

Somewhere a police car siren wailed. Pc Fielding lost what interest he had in Arthur and began to look up and down the street.

"Double yellow line, see," he told Arthur, brusquely. "No parking. At any time. I suggest you telephone…." Arthur spluttered with the righteous indignation of the guilty. "It wasn't actually *on* the line," and he walked back to show the man just where the car had been. "It was just here, by the…."

Then he realized that the policeman wasn't listening. Instead he was stepping out into the road, as the siren came nearer. Then with a squeal of tyres, the police car rounded the corner, and sped towards them. It stopped with an equally high-pitched scream of brakes, and a short dry skid.

The driver poked his head out of the window. "Oi! Terry! You're wanted at the station."

"Right." Arthur's policeman ran back to the van he'd been attempting to start, retrieved his helmet, then sprinted to the police car. Arthur realized that his lifeline to his vanished car was about to be broken.

"Look," he protested, "I want to show you where I parked."

Constable Fielding hardly looked at him. "Sorry, I've got to go. Telephone the police pound."

He got into the police car, and it shot away up the road to the T-junction. Arthur stared after it, disgusted. Come back, George Dixon!

In the police car, Constable Fielding borrowed a cigarette and wanted to know what all the sodding fuss was about.

The driver waited for a gap in the traffic at the junction, and told him that that sod Brunton had drowned himself in the Thames.

Constable Fielding invoked the name of the Deity, and followed that with the observation that now there'd be a vacancy for sergeant.

The driver explained how Brunton had been driving an illegally parked car when, for seemingly no reason, he had abandoned the road for the river.

Constable Fielding asked which car the sergeant had been driving.

The driver described the red Rover and told Fielding its registration number.

Fielding went hot and cold, and then told the driver that the two of them had urgent police work to do.

Back at the kerb, Arthur was joined by Fiona, and they both gazed after the police car.

Arthur was furious. "Bloody typical! Spend all bloody day towing cars away… when there's so much crime about…" and then, without caring who heard him, he bellowed: "Fascists!"

At the T-junction, the police car slammed itself into reverse, and began grinding back down the street towards them.

Arthur stared. Had he shouted that loud? Fiona's hand gripped his arm. He wondered what the law was about calling policemen fascists. He felt rather ill and sweaty.

The car drew to a halt by them, wasting more taxpayers' rubber. Pc Fielding got out and gave Arthur a level stare. Arthur quailed.

"I think you'd better come to the station, sir."

Arthur produced what he thought would be an all-chaps-together type of hearty laugh, but turned out instead to be a nervous please-let-me-off titter.

"Look," he said, "I didn't mean to call you a... you know... anyway, you're right. It was on a yellow line."

Fielding seemed not to hear. At least, he remained unmoved. He held open the car door. "Just get in, would you?"

With the feeling that the gates of the Bloody Tower were closing behind them, Arthur and Fiona climbed in. They sat together in the back seat, holding hands in silence and looking at the spots on Pc Fielding's neck.

A spectacular crash, a sudden death, intense police activity, all these things are bound to draw a crowd.

The to-do at the river bank drew an excellent audience of afternoon time-wasters. It was a spectacular show. A cast of hundreds. Police and ambulance men in force, of course. A Thames police barge. A mobile crane. And, as a special bonus, a team of frogmen.

The action was simple, but full of interest. The frogmen went down and freed the body of the sergeant. It was brought to the surface, beached, stretchered, covered, carried, loaded, and ambulated away to the morgue.

The crane then hooked into a door strut, and winched Arthur's red Rover high out of the water and onto dry land, where it sat and leaked rather sadly. From within it a policeman retrieved the sergeant's flat police cap.

The frogmen stood around getting out of their wet suits, stacking their oxygen cylinders, and lighting cigarettes. And a young constable, who actually had been quite upset by the sight of the sergeant's corpse, covered up his feelings by being brusque and efficient and began to move people on. The show was over.

For the most part, the audience were happy to go. They'd seen enough, and, as the police constable reminded them, they did have homes to go to.

Only one seemed disappointed. He turned and stalked away almost petulantly. Head down, muttering to himself, he found his motorcycle combination, pulled the goggles down from the top of his head, crushed a crash helmet over his beret, started the machine, and roared off in a northerly direction.

Arthur and Fiona sat at a small table of yellow polished wood. The chairs were of similar material and felt potentially uncomfortable. Arthur put his hands under the seat of the chair to shift it forwards, and encountered outgrowths of dried chewing gum. Fiona put her hand on his knee, and, checking that no gum adhered to it, Arthur put his hand on hers.

Facing them, with his arms on the table and his thick hairy fingers locked together, was Detective

Inspector Black.

Behind him, standing slightly to the right, wearing a carefully composed look of intelligent suspicion and going cross-eyed with the effort, was Detective Sergeant Mull.

There was a short silence. Arthur and Fiona waited for the inspector to begin.

Sergeant Mull took the time to compose and prepare himself for the interrogation that was about to commence. The essential thing about being a good detective sergeant was to be of invaluable assistance to the detective inspector during an interrogation.

Partnership, he considered, was the essence of good police detection. Just as no detective sergeant could operate without a detective inspector to lead him, no detective inspector could hope to crack insoluble cases without a bright young detective sergeant at his elbow. It stood to reason.

What's more, all the authorities said the same thing. *All* the authorities. ATV. London Weekend. Thames. Even the BBC. Sergeant Mull mentally raised his hat.

You only had to examine the methods of the successful teams. Reagan and Carter, Maigret and Lucas. Barlow and Watt. Starsky and Hutch. Each acted as a foil to the other. Each augmented the gifts of the other. And so every couple became an unbeatable team. They needed each other.

Thus, mused Sergeant Mull, the essential thing about being a good detective sergeant was to form a similar relationship with the detective inspector.

So, to Inspector Black's experience and rank, he would add his own insight, intelligence, cunning, daring, skill, athleticism, knowledge, foresight, spirit, understanding and humour.

This way they'd be a team, too. An equal partnership, really. Symbiotic. The one leading the investigation in the normal plodding way, the other adding the inspired thought, the flash of genius, the final part of the puzzle from which could be drawn the true and correct conclusion.

And of course, all this was leaving out the question of bravery. The essential thing about being a good detective sergeant was to exhibit such bravery as was needed, as and when it was called for, thus shielding the more senior detective inspector from harm, and of course being awarded the appropriate police medal afterwards.

Sergeant Mull knew that when the moment came he'd be as brave as a lion. His bravery would be the talk of the promotions board. You see, he'd been practising. At home, with his wife. She would creep up behind him and pop paper bags when he least expected it. After three weeks of this, Sergeant Mull could maintain a calm, brave demeanour in the event of any sudden bang. However, he did tend to jump violently at times when nothing whatsoever happened.

Sergeant Mull knew now that his training in bravery was paying off. He could stare at Arthur in the eye and not feel in the least bit afraid, which proved it. In fact, at this very moment, Sergeant Mull felt ready for anything. The essential thing about being a good detective sergeant was to be ready for anything. Sergeant Mull tensed himself on the balls of his feet, and waited.

Detective Inspector Black considered that the essential thing about being a good detective inspector was not to have a great steaming berk like Sergeant Mull as a detective sergeant. He sensed the sergeant tensing himself, heard him breathing heavily through his nose and shuffling his feet. Silly sod!

Black turned his attention to Arthur: "We've found your car, Mr. Harris."

Arthur was relieved, not only that the car had been found, but also that someone had finally spoken. The silence had been intimidating. "So I gather," he said.

"We found it," the inspector continued, "in the Thames."

Arthur couldn't believe it. "In the what?"

Incisive, informative, Sergeant Mull leaned forward. "In the *River* Thames," he explained.

Yes, thought the inspector hopelessly. *That* Thames. Quite correct, sergeant.

Arthur was sincerely shocked. The Thames—that would ruin the upholstery. "How did it get there?" he asked.

That's what we'd like to know," said Inspector Black. "You see, inside it was one of our sergeants."

Arthur stared: "What was he doing in my car?"

Helpful, humorous, Sergeant Mull contributed: "Drowning."

"Is he very... er... very...?"

Mull began to enjoy himself: "Very."

Fiona was bewildered. "But we parked outside a restaurant...."

"On a double yellow line," Mull pointed out sententiously. Black sighed. "Sergeant Brunton was taking it to one of our pounds, where, in order to retrieve it...."

He paused for a fatal second, and Mull cut in incisively: "We take twenty-six of your pounds."

Black turned and looked at Mull. Mull smiled, confident of approval. This time Black's sigh was almost a groan. The door opened, and an anonymous constable entered with a typewritten report, gave it to Black, and left. Black read the report. His expression remained blank.

Arthur found the waiting tedious. "I don't understand," he complained.

Black finished the report. "Well, we do," he said. "Now." And, knowing that it was inviting trouble, he handed the report over his shoulder to Mull.

This time Fiona asked the obvious question: "What's the matter?"

Mull had speed-read the report. Now, his voice swooping and breaking with excitement, he grabbed the chance to tell them.

"I'll tell you what's the matter!" he said. "Up to this moment we were investigating what appeared to be an unfortunate accident. We are now investigating what appears to be an unfortunate murder!"

And his eyes popped with pleasure at the drama of the moment.

"Murder?" Fiona clearly didn't know what Mull was talking about.

Arthur, on the other hand, felt he knew exactly what Mull was talking about. "What are you talking about?" he asked him.

This time Black beat Mull to the punch. "What the sergeant is trying to tell you is that your steering and brakes had been tampered with, and therefore it is a possibility that...."

Once again, a quick pause for breath allowed Mull to get in his oar: "Somebody was trying to kill you!"

Black turned and gave Mull another look. This time Mull caught it and was puzzled. He thought he'd put it rather well.

"Thank you, sergeant," said Black, eliminating

irony from his tone. "It *is* only a possibility, Mr. Harris."

Possibility? thought Arthur. Jesus, it's a bleeding certainty! The odd job man was in full cry! He'd knocked off a police sergeant! Dunked him in the Thames until dead. And there, but for the grace of a double yellow line and a Metropolitan Police crack-down on parking offences, went Arthur.

"But it would help us in our enquiries," Black continued, "if you can think of anyone who bears a grudge against you." Mull, eager to make up lost ground, thought he could help at this point. "Anyone at all—like a jealous colleague at work, or a spiteful neighbour, maybe a sexual indiscretion could have…."

Arthur coughed and squirmed. Fiona looked at him.

"I think he understood the question, Sergeant Mull," said Black heavily.

"A grudge against my husband?" Fiona decided to come to Arthur's defence. That's ridiculous. He's so ordinary." There was a short pause while they all looked at Arthur. Mull and Black wore identical expressions of critical disagreement. Arthur wondered why. After all, he *was* ordinary. Then he remembered that he was wearing his old duffle coat and his woolly hat and the sunglasses. He blushed.

Black said solemnly: "Think hard, Mr. Harris. Is there anyone who might bear a grudge against you? Your reply could save your life."

Oh, if only it could! Arthur began: "Er…."

But what could he say? Could he tell everything? Could he tell them anything? What about just telling them the truth? Mentally he rehearsed the words: a man is trying to kill me because I hired him to do it, because I wanted to commit suicide. That was the truth—but would they believe it? Quite frankly Arthur found it difficult to believe himself. Yet here were the police, it was their duty to stop people killing people. Surely he could tell them.

Arthur shifted forward on his chair. Mull, Black and Fiona all seemed to lean in closer.

But… no, he couldn't! It was too late. Perhaps an hour ago, yes, but not now. Because one of them was dead. The maniac odd job man had killed a copper. And what's more, he'd done it for Arthur. So in the eyes of the most reasonable policeman, he'd be an accessory before the fact. He *couldn't* tell them.

Arthur shifted back in his seat. The others visibly drooped.

And yet—wasn't it the bravest, the wisest course, to come clean? To speak up like a man, to admit the disastrous mistake, to allow the forces of law to take charge, and to be free from the awful expectation of death? Yes, this had to be the way. It was the sensible way, the mature way, the intelligent way! He'd do it. The inspector wanted to know if he knew who would want to kill him? Okay, he'd tell him.

Arthur leaned forward again. The other three tensed themselves. Arthur opened his mouth.

"No," he said.

Nine

Fiona and Arthur were driven back to their flat by Detective Sergeant Mull. Mull performed this chore at the request of Detective Inspector Black, who made the request in order to get Mull out of his hair for a while.

Mull kept his ears open during the trip. The essential thing about being a good detective sergeant is to report to the detective inspector any significant conversations between individuals connected with the case. It would, Mull felt, establish him more favourably in the eyes of Detective Inspector Black if he could return with the news that Arthur had made a whispered confession to his wife, in which he'd admitted a sexual indiscretion with the wife of a Mafia chief, who had sworn not to let food pass his lips before he was revenged. Something of that order, anyway. It would certainly crack the case, and establish Detective Sergeant Mull as an outstanding detective sergeant, even among detective sergeants.

So he listened hard and was disappointed when the journey passed without a word being exchanged between Arthur and Fiona. Instead Arthur spent the time looking out of the rear window of the car, while Fiona talked self-consciously to Mull about the prevalence of double yellow lines in North London.

Mull pulled up in the forecourt. Fiona got out on one side of the car, Arthur on the other. Mull pulled away in a hurry, eager to get back and assist his detective inspector.

Fiona turned around to find Arthur, and he wasn't there. He'd disappeared.

"Arthur?" she called tentatively.

A clump of bushes, part of a rough shrubbery that ran along the front of the flats, rustled. “Shhhhhh!” said one of them.

Fiona sighed, then addressed the bush: “What are you doing?”

“I’m just taking precautions,” said the bush defensively, “like the inspector said.”

“You told the inspector there was no need for precautions.”

“I said there was no need for police protection.”

“Because you said nobody was trying to kill you,” Fiona insisted.

“Right.”

“Then why,” said Fiona, with the air of someone finally winning a particularly stupid argument, “are you hiding in the bushes?”

The bush paused, then shook in an agitated manner. “I *might* be wrong,” it explained.

Fiona groaned. Footsteps crunched on the gravel behind her. She turned quickly. It was Mr. Kemp, taking his corgi for its eighteenth stroll of the day.

“Good evening,” Mr. Kemp said, rather tentatively.

“Hello.” Fiona give him a warm neighbourly smile.

“Who’s that?” the bush demanded.

“It’s the gentleman from upstairs. Mr. Kemp,” Fiona explained.

“Oh,” said the bush tersely. “The one with the yapping corgi.”

Fiona flushed. Her warm neighbourly smile became ragged around the edges. The old man looked worried.

“My husband,” she explained, pointing to the bush.

At this, Mr. Kemp's corgi advanced boldly on the bush, and peed against it. Mr. Kemp moved off across the forecourt, calling to the dog.

Fiona made one last attempt. "Arthur, please!" Then she shrugged, and walked on towards the entrance to the flats. Behind her, all along the wall, the bushes swayed and rustled.

Arthur peeped nervously from the shelter of the last bush. He'd done well so far, he felt. No one had followed them back from the police station, and since then the bushes had provided admirable cover. What's more, at such close proximity, they had a rather pleasant herby smell. Arthur wondered what it was.

Fiona emerged from the entrance and beckoned. Arthur gathered himself, then sprinted out of cover, round, and into the main hall. The way ahead was clear, right up to the lifts. Arthur charged forward.

Something was coming at him from the caretaker's cubby hole!!

Arthur reacted in an instant. Without breaking stride, he threw himself at the shadowy figure. All the frustration, fear and regret of the past hours fused in one all-out ferocious assault. There was nothing scientific about it. No style, no control. He just attacked. He thrust his head into his opponent's face, hammered with his fists, kicked wildly with his feet, did everything he could to smash the shadow into defeat.

It didn't fight back. It just crumbled. Arthur felt a strange savage joy coursing through him. He was winning, he was beating the threat once and for all. He kicked again, and the figure moaned and fell in a heap on the floor, legs slipping wide apart.

Between those legs Arthur saw complete final victory. And he drew back his right foot, ready to plant it there and put the issue beyond doubt. And then....

Thinking about the incident afterwards, Arthur couldn't decide whether it was before he began to kick, or afterwards, that he realized he was beating up the awful caretaker. Perhaps it didn't matter, perhaps nothing could have stopped Arthur from delivering that kick. He was grateful, however, in retrospect, that some instinct of self-preservation prompted the awful caretaker to twist himself slightly, and Arthur's shoe landed instead high on the inside of his upper thigh. Nonetheless, the kick was hard enough to propel the caretaker sharply up against the wall, and his head hit the plaster with a dull "clock."

Arthur stood and looked at what he had done. The front door opened, and he swung round, ready to attack again. It was Mr. Kemp, and his dog, who looked at the scene with mutual astonishment.

Arthur turned back to the caretaker. The man was groaning, and trying to sit up. Arthur held out his hand to him, helped him to his feet. The caretaker staggered, and leaned against the wall. Arthur felt he should say something.

"I'm terribly sorry," he said.

It didn't seem enough. The caretaker gave him a long unfathomable look. Fiona, who had watched the whole thing with one hand clamped over a horrified mouth, now came hurrying up to see if she could help.

Arthur tried again: "I didn't hurt you, did I?"

The caretaker gave a long, tortured groan.

Arthur smiled brightly. "Oh, good," he remarked. Then, deciding that he'd already spent far too long hanging round the exposed and dangerous hall, he made for the lift.

Fiona patted the caretaker awkwardly on the shoulder. "I'm awfully sorry," she told him. "He's had his car stolen."

Arthur was waiting in the lift, anxiously holding the doors open. Fiona walked in, too, then looked back at Mr. Kemp and his corgi, who were now standing nearby.

"Are you coming up?" she asked.

Something close to terror settled on Mr. Kemp's features. He seemed in an instant to grow even older.

"No, thanks," he managed.

As they sped upwards, Fiona rounded angrily on Arthur. "Why did you hit the caretaker?"

Arthur didn't know what to tell her. She couldn't understand. She wasn't walking around under sentence of immediate death. She didn't stand on the brink of the abyss, waiting for some insane little dwarf to push her over. She'd never even met the odd job man. How could he explain? How could he ever explain?

"Why did you hit the caretaker?" she asked again.

Arthur shrugged. "He sneaked up on me."

"He didn't. He just came out of his office."

"In a sneaky way," Arthur insisted. Fiona sniffed, and waited silently for the lift doors to open.

Back in the flat, Fiona went into the bedroom, dropped her bag on the dressing table, and checked her face in the mirror. Then she walked through to the kitchen.

During the time it took her to do that, Arthur put the chain on the door, checked the hall cupboard, checked behind and under all the furniture in the sitting room, checked that no one was hiding in the bath or in the airing cupboard, checked the kitchen including every cupboard in the fitted units, checked the balcony, checked behind the curtains, slipped into the bedroom as Fiona left it and checked under the bed, in the units and behind the curtains, and then he made a quick last tour of the entire flat, before joining Fiona in the kitchen.

The effort left him out of breath, and Fiona thought he looked pale.

She put a hand on his arm. "Oh, do relax, Arthur," she urged. She helped him off with his coat, then told him: "Go and sit down, put your feet up and watch the telly. I'll make you a large drink." And she kissed him on the cheek.

Arthur smiled at her. She was sweet to him. No wonder he'd missed her so desperately.

"Thanks," he said, and went through into the sitting room. Yes, television, he thought. Just the thing. It would help to blot out the fear, and give him the peace he so badly needed. He wondered what was on. Late afternoon—that meant children's programmes. Good—something light, straightforward, amusing, perhaps even informative. As long as it wasn't Blue Peter....

Sighing, stretching with fatigue, Arthur picked up the *Radio Times* from a chair arm. Flicking through the pages while he tried to remember what day it was, he wandered over to the television, bent down to switch it on, and...

... and it wasn't there.

The television had gone.

The bare stand remained. The set itself had gone.

The *Radio Times* dropped from his fingers. The moisture drained from his mouth. The blood drained from his brain. His stomach contracted to a tight little knot of nerves. His breath actually stopped.

Arthur was paralysed with fear.

With a despairing effort, he forced his lungs to work, and they sent out a long loud shuddering breath that rang with terror.

"A... a... aaaaaaagh!"

Fiona rushed in from the kitchen, an unopened bottle of slimming tonic in her hand.

"What is it? What is it?"

Arthur took two deep breaths before he trusted himself to speak. And when he did, his voice still shook. He hoped he was making sense.

"The television. It's gone. Gone... to be repair... because it's broken. That's... why it's not here."

Arthur wished with all his heart that this was true. But he knew that, while he and Fiona had been with the police, the odd job man had been to the flat.

He remembered how the little man had planned to collect it. With a trolley. He must have ridden up in the lift with this trolley, unlocked the flat door with the key that Arthur (Jesus!) had given him, trundled the thing into the sitting room, loaded up the television and the video game—yes, Arthur verified, that had gone too—and rolled the lot out, down and away.

Arthur swallowed. The odd job man had taken payment. Perhaps he considered the job as good as done. Perhaps it was about to be done.

He shook, and Fiona put a sympathetic arm around his shoulders. "My poor love," she said gently. "Look, let's just go to bed early, eh? It's been an exhausting day. You must be dead."

Must I? thought Arthur, plaintively. Must I?

By the time they did go to bed, Arthur had rallied. He recalled his vow to fight back. If he had to go down, then he'd go down fighting. Yes, fighting—and with the only weapon he had. The Samurai sword!

Clearly, he reasoned, he would be at his most vulnerable during darkness. He had to sleep—and at any time the odd job man could enter the flat, using the key which Arthur (Christ!) had given him, and fall on him as he lay defenceless.

But, Arthur told himself, he wouldn't be defenceless if he could just get his hand on that frightening cleaver. If he could wake in time, and just get in a swing with that oriental axe, he'd slice the odd job man up good and proper. He'd lop his head off, he'd de-gut him, he'd hack off his limbs, he'd....

Arthur got a grip on himself. He suddenly felt better. He sensed adrenalin in his veins.

At that moment Fiona was in the bathroom. Arthur, already in pyjamas, found the sword where it still lay, in a corner, and carried it into the bedroom. A picture hung by Arthur's side of the bed—some print of Stubbs he'd never cared for—and he quickly removed it, and hooked the sword up instead. Quickly, he stretched himself on the bed, and reached up with his right hand. Yes, he could easily grasp the handle. Perfect! A sword in the hand was worth two in the sitting room. Or something like that.

He became aware that Fiona had entered the bedroom, and was staring at the sword with undisguised dislike. He busied himself getting into bed.

"What's that doing in here?" she asked.

"I think it looks nice," Arthur told her.

"Yes." She didn't mean it. He didn't care. "Yes, I'll just put the lights out."

Fiona disappeared for a few seconds, then came back into the room, easing her bathrobe off her shoulders. She dropped it on the floor, and stood for a moment, just inside the door. Some faint light from outside the building filtered through and outlined her body through her thin lacy nightdress.

Arthur looked up at her. Again he knew why he

had wanted to die when she left. She smiled, came and sat down on the side of the bed by him. She rested one hand not quite casually on his thigh.

Arthur hesitated. He dearly wanted to make love to Fiona. He knew she felt the same. But the spectre of death would make a third in the bed that night. Was it possible? Could he do it?

Fiona leaned forward and kissed him.

Arthur decided that it was possible, if he could just concentrate on what he was doing. He had to control his thoughts. He had to black out any thought of the odd job man. If he could do this successfully, then he'd be able to make love successfully. But, like some television quiz contestant, he would have to concentrate. Concentrate, concentrate, concentrate.

Her smile gone, Fiona's hand shook slightly as she pulled back the duvet.

That night Arthur won University Challenge, Brain of Britain, and Mastermind.

Later, much later, there was a slight noise from the sitting room.

Arthur was instantly and totally awake.

He listened. Fiona, at his side, slept the sleep of the well-and-truly laid. Then he heard the noise again.

Arthur slid out of bed like a snake, one hand moving with precision to the handle of the Samurai sword. Naked—his pyjamas had been long lost earlier in the night—he stood and listened once again.

There was the noise again!

Arthur wanted to weep. The odd job man had come for him. He wanted to hide, he wanted to crawl under the bed, he wanted to do anything that would save his life. Desperately he wanted to run.

But he could not, and he would not. He gripped

the sword tightly, and it gleamed in the dark. He wasn't helpless, he was armed. And he was a man. Hadn't he already proved that this night? Then he was going to prove it again.

Once more he listened. There it was again....

Assassin-like, Arthur crept across to the sitting room door. All was dark in there. No chance of spotting his target, or making a direct attack. Arthur paused for thought.

The only answer was the scatter-gun principle. The odd job man had to be in there somewhere. If he could swing his sword like a revolving windmill, if he could slice through every square foot of air and floor space in the sitting room, then nothing could live with him.

It was now or never. Arthur breathed in like a Hoover, then whooped like a steam whistle, and moved in like a buzz saw.

The noise woke Fiona. Yells, crashes, grunts, bangs, thumps, shrieks... she lay in bed and listened, and wondered if she was dreaming.

Then she knew that she was awake, and that the hideous din was coming from her sitting room. She felt for Arthur. He wasn't there. Panicking, she slipped naked from the bed and ran to the sitting room door.

It was too dark to see anything clearly. She could just sense great whirling shapes, as the clamour and the crashing continued. She peered desperately—then, kicking herself for being so forgetful, she switched on the light.

Alone in a scene of devastation, a naked Arthur whirled like a demented Dervish.

"Arthur!" she shrieked. "Arthur!"

For a few seconds longer Arthur maintained his deadly momentum. Then, like some clockwork puppet, he slowly unwound. His forays, darts and dashes lost their credibility as he could now see that he was hitting out at nothing. A brief spasm took him behind the sofa in a rush, but there was nothing there. Finally he stood in the centre of the room, waving the sword uncertainly.

Fiona came to him. She wanted to hold him, but he was still too tense, and the sword twitched nervously.

She looked around the room. Lights were smashed, furniture overturned, books strewn, ornaments scattered.

"Oh, my God," she breathed, hand to her mouth.

"He's here!" Arthur trembled.

"Who?"

"Him!"

"Who?"

"The bloke who's trying to kill me."

Fiona shook her head, and tried again to touch him. He was still too taut. "Arthur, there's nobody here. Was it a nightmare?"

Arthur said, with conviction: "The balcony. I closed it before we went to bed."

"I opened it."

"Eh?"

"It was stuffy," she explained. "We always do that if it's warm."

"But… but…." Then Arthur remembered. "I heard a noise!" And he looked at her in triumph.

Then he heard the noise again. From the balcony door. They both heard it, and they both swung round. A loose curtain cord flapped against a window pane.

Arthur capitulated.

Fiona put her arms around him and held him. Then she released him, took the sword from his uncertain hands, placed it on the ground, and put her arms around him again. Trembling, he held her close.

In the next block of flats, away to the right, a middle-aged publishing executive for a group of worthy women's magazines was raiding the fridge for her usual three a.m. snack.

When she had piled her plate with cheese, tomato, celery, cold pork crackling, pâté and a biscuit, she wandered, nibbling, to the window and looked out into the night.

To her surprise, followed quite quickly by her shock and her moral outrage, she saw something disgusting.

In a flat in the next block, naked couples were cavorting. They had the lights on and the curtains open, so they were in full view of anyone glancing casually in their direction.

The publishing executive was outraged. Cheesy-tomato-y crumbs spattered her carpet. She felt compelled to take action.

But by the time she found her binoculars and got back to the window, the naked people had put the light out.

Ten

The next morning was a fine one. When you're a milkman, that means a lot. Wet days, cold days, the job's murder. But at seven o'clock on a sunny morning, when it's just cool enough to keep you on the move, then there's no better occupation.

So John the milkman was in a good mood. He swung his float into the forecourt of the flats, lifted out two loaded crates, and walked cheerfully up to the front door. He didn't whistle, he wasn't very good at it. But he hummed.

Even the sight of the awful caretaker, who answered his buzz on the doorbell, couldn't spoil his mood.

"Morning, squire," he greeted him.

The caretaker grunted. John the milkman dumped two crates down just inside the door and went back for more.

From the door, the awful caretaker watched him until he reached his float. Then, with speedy stealth, he grabbed a pint of milk, a bottle of orange juice, and a chocolate yoghurt from the crates, and hid them in his cubby hole.

While John the milkman was still at his float, and the caretaker was skulking in his cubby hole, a third and unexpected figure joined in this early-morning entr'acte. It was the odd job man, emerging from the same bushes by the front of the flats which had shielded Arthur so successfully the previous evening.

The odd job man checked that John the milkman was still unloading, then slipped in the front door. He sidled past the caretaker's cubby hole, his leather coat making slight swishing noises. The caretaker was busy hiding his yoghurt and didn't hear a thing. The odd job man edged around the corner by the lift, found the door for the emergency fire escape steps, and dived through it.

As the door closed behind him, the caretaker wandered out again into the hall. John the milkman clattered up with more crates, loaded with bread, milk, potatoes and yoghurt.

"Nice day, squire," he commented.

The awful caretaker grunted.

Arthur was dreaming. He had just sliced the odd job man into little pieces with the Samurai sword, and now Detective Inspector Black and the head waiter were asking him to confess, while Detective Sergeant Mull tapped him on the head with an empty wine bottle. Tap tap, he went. Tap tap tap....

Then he was awake. It had been a dream. But the tapping... was still going on!

Arthur reached up for the sword, blessing his foresight in re-hanging it by the bed after last night's debacle. He swung himself out of bed, raised the weapon high over his head, and went rushing through into the sitting room.

Fiona was kneeling in the centre of the room. She was attempting to mend a chair that Arthur had disjointed the night before. She had coated the end of a strut with wood glue, and was now tapping it back into place with Arthur's small hammer. Tap tap....

She looked up at Arthur as he charged in, and sighed, pushing the hair back out of her eyes.

"Not again, Arthur," she told him, as if he were some neighbour's naughty child. "I've just finished clearing up."

Arthur looked around the room and felt embarrassed. A sofa arm looked as if a giant dog had chewed it. The giant dog had also bitten a chunk out of the dining room table—Arthur winced when he remembered the price—and had then gone on to slash and rip at the wallpaper with its huge claws. Arthur winced again. He *hated* wallpapering.

Fiona finished the chair and pushed it into a corner. Wordlessly she stalked into the kitchen. Arthur turned and went to put some clothes on.

John the milkman walked cheerfully up from the floor below, and put two pints of milk down outside Arthur's door. Then he pressed the button for the lift, waited for a few seconds until it came, and got in.

As the twin lift doors closed, the door for the emergency stairs on the same floor opened. The odd job man looked out, checked that all was clear, then tiptoed across the landing to Arthur's door. Soundlessly he picked up the two bottles, turned, and minced back again, and through the emergency doors.

Outside, on the rough iron stairs, he sat down with the bottles between his knees. Carefully he removed the tops. From his pocket he produced a thick glass bottle with a heavy glass stopper—the type of container used in chemistry laboratories and dispensaries.

Then, with a milk bottle in one hand the glass bottle in the other, the odd job man stopped. He had a problem. The milk bottle was already full. He put down the glass bottle on the step and thought about it. He looked around for a place to pour away some of the milk, but nowhere seemed suitable. Then a brainwave struck. He raised the milk bottle to his lips—then stopped again. He put his hand over the top and tipped the bottle to and fro, to mix up the cream. Then, smacking his lips with appreciation, he drank a little milk from each milk bottle.

This left ample room for the contents of the thick glass bottle, which he divided equally between the two milk bottles. Fumes rose from all three bottles, and the odd job man carefully kept his face away from them. Quickly but carefully, he re-stoppered the chemical bottle, and re-capped the milk bottles. He put the chemical bottle in his pocket, took the two milk bottles, and slipped through the door onto the landing again. He put the bottles on the floor by Arthur's door, then went to the lift.

As he reached it, a sharp "ping" announced its imminent and occupied arrival. Like a cornered rat, the odd job man ran for the emergency door and scuttled through it just in time. A little shaken, he hurried down the steps, and reentered the building at the next floor. There he rang for the lift again.

When the lift doors opened on Arthur's floor, they disgorged the awful caretaker. They stayed open, because the caretaker had put the lift on "hold."

The caretaker looked carefully around, to make sure he was unseen. Then he went and stood in front of Arthur's door and stuck his tongue out. He crossed his eyes. He tilted his head, idiot-like, on one side. He put his left thumb to his nose and wiggled his fingers. With the other hand he jerked V-signs into the air. And finally, he blew a quiet but sustained raspberry.

It was an ecstatic moment, and the caretaker stood on one leg and wriggled with the fun of it.

When he spoke, it was with a quiet but enthusiastic venom. "Bloody car's been stolen, has it?" he hissed. "Well, so has your bloody milk!"

And he bent down, picked up one of the bottles,

and slithered back into the lift. He released the "hold," and pressed the button for the ground floor.

One floor down the lift stopped. The odd job man got in. The caretaker hid his bottle of milk behind his back. The odd job man was conscious of his chemical bottle, bulging in his pocket. Neither looked the other in the eye.

"Morning," the caretaker offered.

"Morning." The odd job man make it clear he didn't wish to widen the conversation.

At the next floor the lift, to a sigh from the caretaker, stopped again. John the milkman, carrying two empty crates, got in.

"Morning, squire," he said to the odd job man, ignoring the caretaker.

"Morning."

John the milkman turned to the caretaker. "Only three short," he told him.

The caretaker didn't reply. All three were glad when the lift reached the ground floor.

Still feeling bad about the sitting room, Arthur wandered into the kitchen where Fiona was getting breakfast, and asked her if there was anything he could do.

"You could get the milk." Fiona remained uncharmed.

"Of course." He leaped up to go, but Fiona stopped him.

"Please get it without slicing the door in half or wrenching it off its hinges."

Arthur gave her a weak smile. He hoped she wouldn't notice that the front door was already damaged. Ever since he'd slammed it when she walked out on him.

By the time he got to the door, he'd begun to wish he hadn't volunteered to help. Getting the milk entailed opening the door. Inescapably. And who knew what waited outside the door? The odd job man knew. That's who.

If the odd job man had been outside Arthur's door at that moment, he'd have witnessed a remarkable feat of milk collection.

First the door opened on its security chain. Eyes flashed within the narrow gap. The door closed again. When it reopened, the security chain was off. Very slowly it opened until the gap was about the width of an arm. At that point an arm came through the gap. It moved at great speed, snatched up the milk bottle, then disappeared. The door slammed shut again, missing the fingers by a whisker. There came the rattle of the security chain, then silence.

Inside the flat, Arthur paused to congratulate himself. Then, with a jauntier step than before, he joined Fiona in the kitchen.

"Milk thief's been at it again," he told her, plonking the single bottle on the table. He laughed—"He must be very healthy by now."

Fiona said nothing. They sat at opposite ends of the small breakfast table. Arthur busied himself putting shredded wheat into his bowl and sprinkling it with sugar. Fiona nursed a cup of coffee and stared at him. She waited until he looked up and caught her eye before speaking.

"Arthur?"

"Mmmmmm?"

"Who's trying to kill you?"

Arthur sprinkled sugar over the marmalade.

"Mmmmm?" he said, thinking hard.

"Somebody *is* trying to kill you," Fiona was

positive.

"Nonsense!" said Arthur, with good healthy English contempt for such an absurd notion. And he removed the top from the milk.

Fiona persisted, with good healthy English common-sense. "And you know who it is."

Arthur went for the big lie. "Fiona, if I thought that someone was trying to kill me," he said, with pedantic reasonableness, and pouring milk on his cereal, "and if I knew who they were, I'd tell the police, wouldn't I?"

The Shredded Wheat began to hiss and splutter.

"Good grief!" Arthur was genuinely amazed. "Look at that!"

Fiona glanced at his bowl. "Aren't they supposed to snap, crackle and pop?"

"No, this lot just lie there and soak it up. Funny…." Fumes were rising from the bowl, and Arthur leaned over and sniffed, then jerked his head back.

"It's acid," he told her, incredulously. Then it hit him. "Acid! It's *him!*"

He leaped to his feet, sending bowl, cereal and acid splashing and crashing across the kitchen. Fiona reached out a hand to him, then backed away when she saw the look on his face.

Arthur turned and ran into the sitting room.

He searched frantically around the room. "The sword!" he yelled. "Where's the bloody sword?"

Fiona stood, trembling, at the kitchen door. "Oh, no, Arthur…."

But Arthur wasn't listening. He remembered where the sword was. In the linen basket, in the bedroom. He rushed in and grabbed it. Then, calmer with the weapon now in his hand, he moved menacingly into the hall.

"Arthur, please…." Fiona followed him through, but Arthur impatiently waved her to silence. He advanced on the front door. His hand came down firmly but quietly on the handle. With slow silent deliberation, he turned the knob fully to the left. Then, in one swift devastating movement, he jerked the door open.

And nearly broke his arm. He'd forgotten to undo the security chain. The door jarred to a halt after six inches.

Swearing and fumbling with the chain, Arthur came near to losing the cool sense of dangerous determination which had been his since he put his hand on the sword. But at last he got the damn door open, and hurtled out onto the landing, weapon raised.

It was empty.

The whole floor was empty. Arthur ran up and down the corridor, bristling, but saw no one.

Then he thought of the lift. If the so-called milkman—who was undoubtedly the odd job man in disguise—had dropped off the lethal bottle on his way up, then it was quite possible that by now he would be on his way down.

He ran back to the lift—and knew at once that he had made an inspired guess. From the indicator board he could see that the lift was two floors up. And descending….

Craftily, Arthur pressed the "down" button. Then he positioned himself in front of the doors, legs braced wide apart, sword in both hands high over his head, and he waited.

The lift pinged. Arthur poised. The doors opened.

With a shout of "Aaaagh!" Arthur lunged forward, swinging the sword down. The tip of it dug deep into the metal surround of the lift gates. The handle jarred in his hands. And Arthur found himself staring into the horrified faces of Mr. and Mrs. Kemp.

From somewhere he found a smile. "I'm sorry," he said. "I'm looking for the milkman."

Speechless, possibly struck dumb forever, Mr. and Mrs. Kemp stared back at him. After an eternal pause, the doors closed.

As they met, Arthur realized what a daft thing he'd said. And in way of explanation, he shouted after them. "You see, he only left me one pint."

Left alone, he felt awkward. Then he felt afraid. He looked around. Too many doors, far too many doors. The odd job man could be behind any of them. He turned and sprinted back to his own door, ran inside, and closed it after him.

In the sitting room he told Fiona that he'd seen no one. She took the sword from him and stood it in a corner while Arthur brooded.

Then he had a thought. "He may still be in the building. I'll try the caretaker."

The internal phone was on the wall inside his front door. He dialled the caretaker's extension, then listened impatiently to the buzzing as it rang out far below.

"Come on," he fumed. "Come on!" Stupid old sod, probably playing with himself in the basement, ought to have been pensioned off long ago. "Come *on....*"

Mr. Kemp had been pensioned off some years before. Or, to be strictly accurate, he had pensioned himself off.

By now, he and Mrs. Kemp should have been the owners and occupants of a beautiful old clifftop house near a Cornish fishing village, enjoying their retirement in the sun and the gentle breezes of the channel coast. That was how they'd always planned it.

They had known of the house since 1949. In that year, when rationing began to be phased out and profits from the little corner grocery began to mount, they'd bought an Austin and begun a series of weekend tours. They'd found the house by accident. A wrong turning led them up a dusty private road, which terminated at the house itself. They'd been most embarrassed, but the old retired customs official who owned it lived on his own, and was glad of some surprise company. With pride he had shown them round. It was small, but broad curved windows looked out on a garden that tumbled down to the cliff edge. A further path led in a gentle spiral down through more rocks, until it emerged far below in a small circle of grass totally closed to view from the land, yet trapping all the sun that poured in from above the sea. It was a long way down, but the man who had built the gardens had cut long slow steps into the rock. And he'd made a little paradise.

The Kemps dreamed of the house over the years, and in their minds it became theirs. They visited the customs officer every year, until he died in 1956. By then, what had been a Camden Town corner grocery became a whole block. Unfortunately, with his money tied up in the business Mr. Kemp sadly concluded that the customs officer had died too. soon. He could not make a realistic bid for the house.

For a whole year the Kemps did nothing. But when the summer came round, they made contact with the new owner of the house. But it was not a happy meeting. The man who'd bought it had a terminal illness. The Kemps went away, saddened, but not totally dispirited. After all, if the man was going to die....

Then, in 1967, with the sale of their business going through for an astronomical figure, they drove up the private road once more, and there was the sign they'd been hoping and longing to see: FOR SALE.

The estate agent told them it was already sold. He'd forgotten to remove the board.

They told him it was their dream house.

He told them there was no land title to dreams.

Of course they went to see the new owner. He was an immensely rich farmer from Northamptonshire, whose success at the business of agriculture made Mr. Kemp's commercial achievements appear puny. He told the Kemps, rather loudly, that he had purchased the house as a holiday retreat. He never went abroad, on account of the food, but he liked to move about in Britain, and have a home wherever he went.

Mr. Kemp explained how he and his wife had always admired the house, and then made him a very agreeable offer for it. The farmer refused to discuss it. Mr. Kemp told his wife on their way home, with a humour surprising for such a straight businessman, that at last he knew why there was such a rural flavour to the saying about the dog and the manger.

They looked at other houses, and while they looked they took the flat in Arthur's block. As a temporary measure. But none of the homes they saw pleased them. And as the sixties wore on into the seventies, for both the Kemps and the century, they looked at less and less. Gradually the fact that they actually continued to live in central London became a source of pride. No matter how much it might change, London would always be home for them. It was almost a relief when Mr. Kemp's eyesight made it necessary to sell the last car—a Jaguar by then—and trips out to the country became such a nuisance to organize. They enjoyed a new contentment, marred only when they allowed themselves to remember the house on the Cornish coast.

And yet there were times when Mr. and Mrs. Kemp wondered if they'd made the right decision. Such strange people came to live in the flats these days. Really, quite disturbing.

The other afternoon some of them had had such an awful row, shouting and slamming doors. And yesterday afternoon Mr. Harris from three floors below had behaved most strangely in the car park, and then assaulted the caretaker. Mr. Kemp, who had witnessed these incidents, had been quite upset, and so this morning Mrs. Kemp decided to take him along to the doctor and see if he needed a nerve tonic.

It was perhaps a pity that they chose to make use of the lift when they did. The resulting confrontation with an unstable Arthur did nothing to tranquillize either of them. When the lift finally reached the ground floor, Mrs. Kemp was trembling, ashen-faced, near collapse. And she was by far the fitter of the two.

Holding Mr. Kemp's arm with care, she took him out of the lift, and together they leaned against the wall and tried to catch their breath. Mrs. Kemp was quite clear about what they should do. There was no alternative. They must make the ultimate protest, enact the final sanction.

"We must speak to the caretaker!"

Arthur gave up. He told Fiona everything. *Everything.*

He never felt so stupid.

Fiona looked at him as if he had gone suddenly

and completely bald. She was sitting in an armchair. Arthur sat opposite on the sofa. He gave her a little-boy-lost smile.

Fiona said, slowly: "You… hired… someone… to kill you?"

Arthur remembered how once he'd reported a car accident to the police. He could hear again the tone of the desk sergeant's voice: "You left your car unlocked with the engine running on a hill with the handbrake off…?"

"Yes," he admitted. Then and now.

Fiona squeaked with incredulity. "And you did that because I left you?"

"Yes… you see, I thought…." Arthur had begun a feeble defence of his sanity, but then he was bowled over as Fiona flung herself at him. Her arms went round his neck, and she began soaking his face with kisses and tears. He'd pleased her, Arthur realized. By luring the odd job assassin, he'd actually made her happy. He blew some of her hair out of his mouth and grimaced to himself. It might have been simpler, in the long run, to buy her two dozen long-stemmed roses.

He put his arms on her shoulders, and held her away from him. "You're missing the point," he said seriously. "He is *still* out to… to get me!"

Fiona smiled. She had the answer. She knew what to do. "Tell him not to."

Creeping Jesu, didn't anyone understand? Arthur felt his voice rising in an unsteady curve, as he tried once more to explain.

"I've no idea where he is, or who he is… nothing about him! I don't even know his name. He's mad. Even if I do get to him, I made him swear to ignore anything I say or do!"

She began to understand. Arthur knew, because

he recognized the beginnings of fear and panic in her eyes. He'd seen the same look, only fully matured, in his shaving mirror. But Fiona still hadn't quite grasped the entire tragedy, as her next remark revealed.

"Tell the police!"

Arthur groaned. "Oh, yes… excuse me, officer. I've arranged to have myself bumped off but I've changed my mind. Can you muster all your constabulary and stop the man. Oh, by the way, he's already killed one of your sergeants. My fault entirely."

He felt ashamed then of his sarcasm, but Fiona was too shocked by the situation to protest. She just stared at him, her eyes wide.

"What can we do?" she asked.

Arthur shrugged. "Wait until he gets fed up failing, or… wait until he succeeds."

A hopeless depression descended on both of them.

Mr. and Mrs. Kemp hobbled determinedly along the hall and into the caretaker's cubby hole. The man was sitting with his back to them. He might have been dozing.

Despite the problem of keeping Mr. Kemp upright and, despite her own tattered nerve-ends, Mrs. Kemp was shocked to see that the caretaker had dropped a bottle of milk on the floor and smashed it. Such a waste. Then she noticed that the milk was smoking. How strange.

She put a hand on the caretaker's shoulder. "I say… Mr. Caretaker?"

The man's swivel chair swung round. His eyes stared sightlessly. The front of his uniform was burned and still smouldered. A wisp of smoke rose from his open mouth.

Mrs. Kemp screamed and raised both hands to her face. Unsupported, Mr. Kemp folded neatly into the caretaker's waste paper basket.

Eleven

"What can we do?" Fiona asked.

Arthur wished she wouldn't. She'd asked the same question twelve times in the past half hour, ever since he'd told her about the odd job man. She'd asked it desperately, she'd asked it plaintively, she'd asked it angrily, she'd asked it thought fully, she'd asked it pragmatically, sometimes she'd just asked it with no expression whatsoever. Quite frankly, Arthur thought the question was counter-productive. And, Arthur told himself, although he loved Fiona for her mind as well as her body, and had always thought of her as an intelligent companion and a fine conversationalist, if she said "What can we do?" once more, he would ask her a question himself. He would ask her why she didn't shut her fat mouth.

Fiona said: "I know what we can do."

"Why don't you shut...." began Arthur, then caught himself just in time. "What?"

"Phone Tony! We'll phone Tony!"

Tony! Of course! That was a great idea. Tony, his best, his oldest friend, Arthur thought fondly. He was a real mate. He'd help. He wouldn't let a friend down. Arthur remembered how he'd rung old Tony on the night Fiona left. It had been good to have a real friend to talk to, on a night like that—although for the life of him he couldn't remember what they'd said to each other. Well, maybe old Tony could help them now. He wouldn't let him down. Not old Tony.

Fiona picked up the phone and dialled.

"Tony? It's Fiona...." She paused, clicking her tongue impatiently while Tony must have said something. Then she interrupted him, abruptly. "Listen—we need help. Don't ask any questions, just get round here. Please."

She put the phone down. Arthur wondered why she'd flushed. "He's coming," she said shortly.

Arthur got up, restlessly, and strode across the sitting room. When he reached the wall there was nowhere else to go, so he turned around and started back. He was halfway there when the doorbell rang.

Arthur froze in mid-stride and looked down at Fiona. Tony? No, it couldn't be. Not yet.

"Oh, my God!" Arthur had to clench his sphincter. "He's back!" He whipped around and scrabbled in the corner for the sword. The blood roared in his ears.

Fiona got up with determination. "I'll answer it," she said, walking towards the hall. "He's not after me."

Arthur wanted to laugh. "He wasn't after the policeman either," he pointed out.

Fiona paused at the door into the hall and turned back to Arthur. "Now listen," she said. She used a low urgent tone that Arthur had only rarely heard. He listened.

"If it *is* him," she said, "I'll let him in. You grab him from behind. Then we'll tell him the job's off. Right?"

Arthur nodded. It sounded right.

"Right." She turned, then paused again. "What does he look like?"

What does he look like? Arthur's thoughts raced in a wild jumble through his mind. He looks like a raving loony, that's what he looks like. His eyes flashed like signal lamps and his teeth point inwards and his hair is brown with black streaks and one of his ears is bigger than the other and he hasn't got any eyebrows and his nose is so stuck up you can see half an inch up it and his fingernails are clean and cut into points and he's got a larynx like a pineapple and a spot on his chin that he picks and… or was he imagining all that?

Fiona was still waiting.

Arthur gestured helplessly. "Well, he's sort of…" and he bent his knees and waddled like the odd job man, "and he's got, well, mad eyes." And he rolled his eyes at her.

Fiona clearly didn't believe that such a creature had ever existed. There was no time for more explanations. The bell rang again.

Quickly Arthur ran to the front door and stood so that when it opened he would be hidden behind it. He raised the sword above his head. The action was becoming familiar, he thought. If he ever got out of this mess, he would set up as an executioner himself. Fully experienced.

He nodded to Fiona, who took a deep breath, put on a small smile and opened the door.

Arthur held his breath….

Detective Sergeant Mull thought it ought to be him standing in front of Detective Inspector Black at the door, and not the other way round. How could he take a bullet gallantly in the shoulder, thus saving the detective inspector from injury and enabling him to make an arrest, when any bullet reaching him would first have to pass completely through the detective inspector? Of course, if he'd been tall and lean, like Carter on television, then he might have been able to lean over the inspector and shove a shoulder in the way in the nick of time—but as he was, it couldn't be denied some three inches shorter and considerably slighter than the inspector, it was quite useless to speculate.

Anyway, thought Mull, the whole approach was wrong This was the flat of the Harris man. The day before that man had been connected with the drowning of a police sergeant. Today he was connected with the death of a caretaker. They shouldn't be standing there at the door politely ringing the bell. They should be charging down the corridor, throwing their shoulders against the door, bursting in, pistols at the ready. Going in hard. However, it was clear that Detective Inspector Black had no intention of adopting that approach, and Mull knew he could hardly adopt it or his own, firstly because he lacked the rank, and secondly because, as he'd already admitted to himself, he was short and slim and tended to bounce off doors, rather than crash through them.

As it turned out, there was no bullet to take in the shoulder. The door was opened by the Harris man's wife. Mull shrugged mentally. Next time. Next time.

Fiona's manner was both heavily surprised and extremely deliberate. "Oh," she exclaimed. And then, after a long pause, "Inspector… Black… and Sergeant…."

Mull couldn't wait. "Mull," he said smartly, thinking how splendid his name sounded when he said it out loud. "Good morning, Mrs. Harris."

Black half turned. The temptation to tell Mull to wait outside was almost irresistible. He fought it.

"May we have a word with you and your husband?" he asked Fiona.

"Of course." Fiona paused. Then—"Come in."

She glanced over her shoulder, then finally opened the door. Inspector Black followed her through the hall. Mull followed him eagerly and stepped on his heel.

Fiona had played for time, and won. Arthur

found no problem in darting back into the sitting room, where he could walk up and down and whistle slightly and look relaxed and casual.

As Fiona led the policemen in, he suddenly realized that his relaxed and casual look was ruined by the sword in his hand. At once he raised the thing and deliberately chopped off one of the lower leaves of Fiona's prize rubber plant. Carefully ignoring Black and Mull, he then chopped off another.

Black interrupted him: "Hello, sir."

Arthur painted surprise on his face and looked up. "Ah...." he began, forcing a relaxed and casual laugh. He gave the sword a slight wave. "Pruning...." Thank heaven the rubber plant had survived the carnage of the previous night.

Black's face twitched with suspicion. He turned and shot a keen glance at Mull. Mull gave him a bright smile. Black sighed.

Arthur imagined that the pot containing the rubber plant was the odd job man's head and thrust the sword deep into it. Then he turned back to the policemen and invited them to sit down.

Black chose a comfortable armchair. Mull preferred an upright chair from which he could spring to instant action. Across the coffee table from them, Arthur and Fiona sat together on the sofa.

"I'll get straight to the point, Mr. Harris, Mrs. Harris," said Black.

"Yes?" Arthur wondered what it was. The car again, it had to be. Or some stupid trifle, blown up out of all importance.

Black began: "Are you acquainted with the caretaker of this block?"

Arthur wanted to laugh. It was some stupid trifle blown up out of all importance. But he kept his face straight, and asked: "Oh, yes. What's he done?"

Mull loomed forward in his chair, his face working. He couldn't miss a chance like this. The second in two days, too. Fantastic! Clearly and loudly he answered Arthur's question: "He's died! That's what he's done!"

Arthur was staggered. What was it with death? *Everyone* was doing it.

Black said, matter-of-factly: "Drank a bottle of gold top milk laced with hydrocyanic acid."

Milk! Acid! Arthur heard a shrill little scream. Was it Fiona, or had he screamed himself? He glanced at her. She had lost all her colour, and her fist was clamped against her lips. If Arthur didn't say something quick, then she would And she'd certainly say the wrong thing. He spoke up quickly:

"What... er... what... er... what... wha... what... er...."

Black looked at him politely. "Sir?"

Shit, now he *had* to say something. And something sensible, too. Desperately, he began, "What was..." and then inspiration struck. "What was the name of that acid again?"

"Hydrocyanic." Black enunciated each of the five syllables with equal weight.

"Oh...."

Mull decided it was time he asked a question. "Why?"

"Oh, nothing...." Arthur attempted the airy wave of the interested but uninvolved spectator. "Just... never heard of it before." He swallowed what seemed an unusual amount of saliva in his mouth, and decided to spread the load a little. "You, darling?" he asked Fiona.

By now she too was composed. "No," she said,

like a society hostess denying knowledge of social security benefits.

Mull and Black exchanged a look that didn't help either of them.

Mull had been practising his next question to himself. He now drew himself up like a latter-day Roundhead inquisitor, and asked it: "When did you last see your caretaker?"

"Er...." Arthur's brain was sagging under the strain. He knew that his answer mustn't incriminate him in any way, but he wasn't too clear about what it was he didn't want to be incriminated in. In any case, he genuinely couldn't remember when he had last seen his caretaker, so he didn't dare lie in case he told the truth, and he didn't dare tell the truth in case it was a lie. "Er...," he said again.

Fiona gave Mull his answer: "Last night, after we'd seen you."

Black's eyes narrowed. "Notice anything unusual about him?"

Arthur felt safe. "No," he said.

"Anything out of the ordinary occur?"

Arthur relaxed. "No," he said with confidence. "No...." He felt he had reached dry ground at last.

Black immediately threw him back in the deep end. "A resident of this block states that he saw you assaulting the caretaker."

Oh, God! "Oh, yes... yes." Old Mr. Kemp must have grassed. "That's right."

"Isn't *that* a bit unusual and out of the ordinary, sir?" Black exercised his skill at police sarcasm with devastating effect. "Or is it a sort of regular occurrence?"

Arthur came clean: "He opened the door of his office rather suddenly, as I was passing."

"So you assaulted him," Mull said heavily.

"You did tell him to take precautions," Fiona protested "in case someone was trying to… trying to… well…."

Her nerve failed her. It didn't fail Mull. "Kill him," he prompted gleefully.

Arthur winced. Black winced. Fiona, in a very small voice, said: "Yes."

Black put his head slightly on one side and looked at Arthur quizzically. "Did you think that the caretaker was trying to kill you?"

"Yes… er… no… I mean… yes…." Jesus! He couldn't even remember what the right answer was. "Yes!"

"Which is it, sir?" Black asked, in almost a kindly manner "Yes, no, yes or yes?"

Fiona got swiftly to her feet, beamed around at them and rubbed her hands together, for all the world like some hostess about to suggest a hearty round of wife-swapping "I've made some coffee," she announced. "Would you like some?"

Arthur loved her. She'd always had this uncanny knack for the *non sequitur*. She'd have been playing deck quoits when the *Titanic* sank.

"Yes!" he said enthusiastically. He watched her wall briskly off into the kitchen—and, contrarily, he felt she'd abandoned him, left him helpless.

Detective Sergeant Mull must have felt it too, because he came roaring in like a tank: "Alia! So you thought he *was* trying to kill you?"

"No," Arthur protested.

"You just said 'yes.'"

"To coffee!"

Black sighed. He'd seen that one coming. Mull, who hadn't, got up and began walking around the room, looking vaguely for something he could kick.

Arthur thought he ought to say something. "Look," he began hesitantly, "after the car business I was a bit on edge. The caretaker startled me. I did apologize to him after I'd hit him."

"How considerate of you." Mull's police sarcasm was a raw, untempered weapon, with none of the cutting edge and savage point wielded by Black. Indeed, it was so poor, it hardly rated as sarcasm at all. Mull knew it, too. Especially when Arthur gave him a warm smile of appreciation.

Mull continued his pacing. There was something about that sitting room that aroused his suspicions. He threw his police powers of observation into high gear. Yes—the arm of the sofa. Mutilated. The dining room table. A big chunk missing. The wall. Slashed and cut.

Observation: severe damage to otherwise immaculate posh room.

Conclusion:...

Mull wondered. This was the tricky bit about police investigation. Yet the essential thing about being a good detective sergeant was to draw the correct conclusion from accurate observation. Mull looked again at the damage. Slowly, but inescapably, he drew his conclusion.

The sofa, the table and the wallpaper had all been attacked by a giant dog.

Black didn't look at Mull as he meandered about the room. But he could sense that the man was thinking. This was very bad news. Mull was problem enough when he merely responded to impulse and stimulus. In that condition one could normally make a guess at which way the man would make a fool of himself. But when Mull began thinking, then he might shoot off at any tangent, say anything, do anything. If

Black had been younger, he mused, he might have enjoyed the suspense. As it was... well, perhaps he'd better say something placatory, and hope that Mull kept his mouth shut.

"Sorry about all the questions," he told Arthur. "But you do realize we're investigating two mysterious deaths and... well... you're the only lead we've got."

Arthur nodded, like a good citizen. "It's all a mystery to me," he lied.

"Just out of curiosity, sir...." Mull went into his impression of a very laid-back Maigret, "Just out of curiosity, these marks on the wall..." he touched it, "this..." He touched the ruined table, "and this...." He touched the mutilated sofa arm. "How did they happen?"

Arthur's thoughts raced again. Perhaps he should claim that it had all been caused by a giant dog. But, no—the police weren't stupid enough to believe that. He decided on a half-truth.

"I did that with the sword," and he indicated the Samurai weapon, sticking up in the plant pot, "practising—to keep fit."

"In here?" Mull sneered with disbelief. The man was clearly trying to conceal the truth about the giant dog. Now if only he could establish the connection between the tampered car brakes, the caretaker, the acid in the milk, and the giant dog

"There's not enough space in the bedroom," Arthur explained.

Mull gave Black a look of significance. We've got him cornered here, it said. Black gave Mull a look of significance. Before he could understand what it said, Mull saw that Fiona was coming in with a tray of coffee.

She'd heard the latest exchange. "I told him not

to," she put in.

Then Mull remembered something. "Two residents of the block saw you rushing about the corridor this morning, brandishing that weapon."

"Oh...." It was a good point, it needed a good answer. Arthur found that he had made up too many answers already that morning. The well of inspiration had run dry.

Fiona, with the air of someone pointing out the obvious, said tartly: "That's because I won't let him practise in here."

Mull's mouth hung open. What now? There had to be a next question. A real blisterer was required. Something to smash aside the wall of lies, to demoralize the suspect, to reach out and expose the truth. Trouble was, they seemed to have come round in a circle with that bloody sword. Now if it had been a giant dog....

Fiona sat down and poured coffee into cups. "Help yourselves to milk and sugar," she said brightly.

Black leaned forward, took a cup, and put it on the coffee table in front of him. "Suicide," he said.

"What?" Arthur gulped.

"... *is* a possibility in the case of the caretaker," Black continued, almost philosophically. "But acid? It's such a diabolical way to do it."

Still musing, he picked up the milk jug.

Acid... milk....

Arthur made the connection, and screamed. "Aaaaagh!" One hand shot desperately towards Black.

Black looked at him mildly, and put the milk down. Arthur collapsed with relief.

"You've thought of something?" Black enquired.

"Yes." It was almost a sob.

Mull shot into action. He grabbed his notebook, whipping it out of his top jacket pocket. With it came two blue ball-point pens, a bus ticket, a nail file, a book of matches from the Flamingo night club, a used tissue, a biscuit, a nasal inhaler, and a quantity of fluff. Mull bent, face red, and picked the items up. He had to scrabble under an armchair for the nasal inhaler. Black watched him in silence, with a small smile on his lips. Finally, when Mull was ready, notebook and pen poised, Black turned back to Arthur.

"Yes?"

"Yes." Arthur had thought long and hard, and had come up with an answer. "Brandy."

He got up and walked across to the drinks cabinet, found a bottle of Courvoisier, and brought it back. Fiona looked up at him, puzzled. Arthur stared back at her, trying to say, "The milk's got acid in it, you dumb bird!" in one facial expression. He failed.

Mull stuffed his notebook away, and sat down again. A suspicion was slowly forming in his mind. "What about the brandy, sir?" he asked.

"That's what I say!" Arthur pretended he was hosting a riotous party. "What about the brandy?"

And quickly, before anyone could say anything, he topped up Black's coffee with the brandy bottle.

Black was surprised but pleased. He liked brandy in coffee. "Thank you," he said.

Arthur turned with an eager smile to Mull, and was about to pour when Mull put a big pink hand over his cup.

"Not for me, thanks."

Arthur looked at him. Mull looked back, levelly. "A Scotsman?" Arthur asked brightly. "Of course. I'll get the whisky."

Mull stopped him with one word: "Milk."

"Vodka!" The sweat ran into Arthur's eyes.

"Not while I'm on duty, sir." Mull savoured the

phrase. It reeked of Barlow, that one. And it made Black look like a soak. "Milk, please," he said, and reached for the jug.

Arthur got there first. He grabbed the milk jug, and held it up just out of Mull's reach. Mull stretched a little further. Arthur held the jug higher. He could sense Fiona twisting on the sofa beside him, trying to tell him something, but he ignored her. The milk jug was now above his head. Mull was off his chair in an awkward crouch, reaching for it.

"Arthur!" Fiona's voice held painful appeal. Arthur glanced round at her.

"May I?" Mull straightened up and grabbed the jug. Arthur felt his wrist twist painfully, and then the jug was gone. Mull had it safe.

Mull felt triumphant. Now he was really on to something. This was detection. There was something wrong with that milk. The man Harris was behaving like a lunatic. There *had* to be something wrong with the milk.

Fiona told him: "He doesn't want you to have any...."

Mull chose his words with care. He wished to remember exactly what was said, for the time when he came to write up his glowing report. "Why's that?" he asked finally.

There was no answer. He looked again at the milk. It seemed normal. That was suspicious, in itself. He sniffed it. Hmmm... nothing he could put his finger on. So Sergeant Mull took his finger, and gently pushed it down into the jug.

For about the tenth time that morning, Arthur gave up. This had to be it. A scream of pain, accusations, exposure, humiliation, punishment... the only slight consolation that the man about to be burned was the idiot Mull. He waited, eyes shut.

Mull dipped his finger in the milk. He pulled it out, stuck it in his mouth.

Fiona finished her previous sentence, with a rush: "... because it's condensed."

Arthur opened his eyes. What?

"What?" said Mull. She was right. The stuff was condensed.

Fiona gave Arthur the fond public smile of a wife who loves everything about her husband, even his little peculiarities.

"He hates giving guests condensed milk," she told the policeman.

Arthur joined in: "But we love it."

Mull's finger was sticky. He put it back in his mouth and sucked. They'd come round in a bloody circle again. One moment his detection was proceeding along a straight line, with the truth just around the corner. So to speak. Then the next moment they were back where they started.

He took his finger out of his mouth again. First the sword. Then the milk. Was it possible he'd been wrong all along? A thought struck him. Perhaps the giant dog was really the answer, after all.

He turned to Detective Inspector Black, eagerly, to mention it. Then he stopped. Black was gazing at the ceiling with such despair that only the whites of his eyes were visible.

The ambulance men who came to get the awful caretaker's body did a quick job on old Mr. Kemp while they were at it. They stuck some plaster across a cut on his balding head. The cut had been sustained not when he fell into the caretaker's litter basket, but later, when he'd been lifted out by a police constable, stood on his feet, and allowed to crash backwards into a coat hook.

But he was better now. Public attention is a great healer. And, while the ambulance men lit a cigarette or two and waited for the police to finish with the body, he and Mrs. Kemp held court to other flat-dwellers. They talked a great deal about the expression on the caretaker's face, and the steaming milk, and they completely forgot to mention the incident which led to the discovery—the appearance of the mad Mr. Harris with the sword.

As they talked, the odd job man trundled slowly past the flats on his motorcycle combination.

His eyes gleamed behind his goggles as he saw the ambulance and the activity, and he allowed the combination to splutter to a halt a little further down the road. Then, keeping his helmet on as an additional disguise, he wandered back up the road and into the forecourt.

He approached an ambulance man. "What's up, then?"

"Been an accident."

The odd job man grinned. "Oh, dear. What sort?"

"Some bloke swallowed some dangerous chemical or something."

"Oh... ooo... er...." The odd job man rose on his toes. "Hurt badly?"

"Naw."

He sank back. "Oh."

"Killed him."

"Oh, dear... oh, dear... oh, dear...." The odd job man rose on one foot and turned round in a complete circle. The ambulance man, accustomed to shock reactions, took no notice.

"Caretaker of the flats here," he volunteered.

The odd job man stopped turning. "That's who

found him?"

"Naw. That's who died."

The odd job man walked back to his combination. He kicked petulantly at the sidecar. Then he got on and rode away into the traffic.

Twelve

The police had gone. Arthur poured three inches of scotch into his glass, sat down in his armchair, and went into mourning for the awful caretaker.

"The caretaker," he said softly, hardly believing it. "The poor old… caretaker."

He felt the man's death to be a close and personal loss. It was hardly possible that lie had gone. He remembered some of the caretaker's little habits. The way he scratched his ears with matchsticks. The sound of the metal tips on his boots on the concrete. His greetings, whenever it rained: "Wet enough for you, sir?" He remembered the man's intelligence. How once the lock on Arthur's door had jammed, trapping him alone in the flat, and how he'd buzzed down to the caretaker, and told him that the lock was stuck, and how the caretaker had replied with the greatest suspicion: "In that case how did you get in?" It was incidents like this he remembered. Of course, as a caretaker, even as a man, he had not been perfect. He had been scruffy, for instance. His jacket was held together with paperclips, for want of buttons. His tie held up his trousers. He cut his own hair. Yes, if the truth were told, he was scruffy. He was also smelly. And nosy. And impertinent. And dirty. But these things were not his fault, he couldn't help them. Well… perhaps, yes, he could help them. But just because a man is scruffy, smelly, nosy, impertinent and dirty—and inefficient, the caretaker had been terribly inefficient, there'd been a dog turd on the doormat for three days once—yes, all right, just because he was scruffy, smelly, nosy, impertinent, dirty and inefficient, was that a good reason for him to die? A good *enough* reason, anyway?

Arthur drank deep from his scotch. Why did the caretaker have to die? Why?

"He was a thief!" Fiona was not in mourning.

Arthur hadn't realized he'd been thinking aloud. "But..," he said, "that poor old caretaker...."

"Look!" Fiona was at her most schoolmistressish. "If he hadn't been a thief, he wouldn't be dead."

True, thought Arthur. "True," he said. "And then, I would."

"Exactly."

Arthur came out of mourning for the awful caretaker. Better him than me, he thought. And it meant there'd be a new caretaker. That was quite a reasonable prospect. Perhaps this time they'd get one who could make the boiler work before December each year. Or one without a snuffle. Or one who didn't spit. Or one who—yes, please, please, one who didn't whistle through his teeth. He took another deep swig of scotch. Yes, soon it might even be a pleasure to walk through the front entrance hall and wish the uniformed figure a cheerful good morning, without getting some wingeing complaint or smart-alec reply in return. Arthur felt suddenly cheerful. Good riddance to the awful caretaker. And thanks, in a way, to the odd job man. He might be a bit inaccurate, but at least he was lethal.

Arthur looked up and smiled at Fiona, but she remained serious. "But.. ," she began, troubled.

Arthur nodded. His momentary euphoria faded rapidly, and the old chill descended once again.

"But," he agreed, "it's only a matter of time before he has another go at me."

Silently, Fiona sat down on the arm of his chair, and took his hand and held it tightly.

Tony's Citroen CX2400 swept into the forecourt, and straight into a narrow parking space, without hesitation. Tony knew without a doubt that he was the best non-competitive driver in North London, but it was nice to prove it occasionally.

He was equally warmed to see that the Citroen was undoubtedly the best car in the entire forecourt. Well... there was one Rolls. But Tony didn't count British cars.

He also noticed the ambulance, the police cars, and the general hubbub. He sighed. Perhaps Arthur had tried to kill himself after all. Then he shrugged. The trouble with saying that the ones who threaten to do it never do is that then they very often *do* do it. Just to spite you. He wondered idly if Arthur had succeeded. And if he had, how long would it take for Fiona to snap out of conventional grief, and give him a bang. Not too long, he hoped.

He walked briskly into the front entrance hall.

Inside the hall, just past the door to the caretaker's cubby hole, Detective Sergeant Mull stood and observed.

Black had gone back into the cubby hole to talk to the forensic boys. Mull decided to wait in the hall. If he crowded into the cubby hole, he might get in Black's way, and the essential thing about being a good detective sergeant is not to get in the way of the detective inspector. In any case, he'd just as well not go into the cubby hole, because the police photographer was still taking pictures of the caretaker, and Detective Sergeant Mull had seen the dead face with the burnt lips and he did not wish to see it again if he could avoid it.

Thus he was in an excellent position to observe Tony when he walked in the door. He was a tall, slim, successful-looking young man, and immediately his automatic instinct to detect took over. A professional man, he decided. Quite possibly a lawyer. Yes, a criminal lawyer, he decided. He speculated a little more. Perhaps a lawyer called in by the man Harris. No, not as a professional adviser. Not yet. But then, he might be a personal friend. Mull's heart beat a little faster. This might be a very interesting piece of deduction indeed!

Then, as Tony paused to peer into the cubby hole at all the police activity, Sergeant Mull remembered his other detections and deductions of the morning—the damage to the sitting room, the milk, and his heart sank. He was probably wrong again. No, he was almost certainly wrong again. Lawyer? The man was probably a civil engineer. Friend of Harris's? He probably lived in the place. Mull sneered at himself. Detective? More like defective. He could almost hear the gurgle as his self-confidence drained away. Lawyer indeed!

Three days later, in the middle of the night, Mull sat up in bed and whistled. He'd just seen Tony's face in a dream. And he'd realized that he had seen him in the past. In fact, he knew the face well. He'd seen it from the witness box, as it asked him searching questions from beneath a neat white wig. No wonder he'd deduced that the man was a criminal lawyer. While his wife watched in astonishment, Detective Sergeant Mull got out of bed and hit himself with a shoe.

But now, sunk in depression, he watched dully as Tony satisfied his curiosity about the cubby hole, and strode on towards the lift. Mull was so buried in his thoughts that he made no move to get out of Tony's way.

They met in the middle of the hall. Mull woke up

and moved to his left just as Tony moved in the same direction. After a pause they both moved back again. Then Tony sighed, put his hands on Mull's arms, moved him to one side, and stepped past.

As Mull watched him go, he stepped backwards towards the cubby hole and walked slap into Detective Inspector Black.

The doorbell rang.

Arthur sank into his chair with fright. Fiona rose briskly to her feet.

Arthur stared. "What are you doing!" It was more of an exclamation than a question.

"Answering the door," Fiona told him with exasperation. "It'll be Tony."

Arthur left the chair like a rocket, and grabbed Fiona by the hips to stop her.

"How can you tell from a doorbell?" he asked.

The desperate logic of the question got through to Fiona, and so, quietly and holding hands, they tiptoed out into the hall and stood at the door, listening.

The bell rang again. Arthur jumped and Fiona squeaked.

Arthur spoke first: "Hello?"

They both heard Tony quite clearly. "Hello!"

"Who's that?" Arthur asked.

Fiona answered him. "Tony." I told you so, her tone said.

"It might not be," Arthur argued.

"It *is* Tony," said Tony.

"There!" Fiona was triumphant.

"He might have heard you saying it."

"Arthur?" Tony now sounded irritable.

"It's him!" Fiona lost patience, unhooked the security chain, and opened the door. Arthur dived behind it for cover.

Tony came in, angrily pushing past Fiona.

"What the hell's going on here?" he demanded. "The place is crawling with police."

He turned and nearly fell over Arthur, as he emerged from his hiding place. Tony looked from Arthur to Fiona, then back to Arthur. Fiona looked at Arthur. There was a short silence. Arthur decided that he must tell his friend everything, the whole issue, as plainly and honestly" as possible, no trying to minimize anything, just tell it like it is.

He took a deep breath and told Tony: "I've got a little bit of a problem."

Fiona looked at the ceiling and sighed.

The full weight of police scientific investigation had a full and weighty go at the caretaker and his cubby hole, and departed. The body, covered now by a red blanket, waited on the floor. Mull felt better about that, and didn't mind at all when Black led the way back in.

Black was examining the array of dairy produce which been discovered in the caretaker's cupboard. Mull stood behind him and waited. The inspector took some time over each item, and Mull, in the presence of his experienced superior, began to feel some of his confidence returning. After all, it had been some time since Black last said anything derogatory to him. To be truthful, it had been some time since Black said anything at all to him. Nonetheless, here they were, working as a team again. Mull decided to make no comment at the moment. This was a time to be silent. The essential thing about being a good detective sergeant is not to say anything unless you have something really good to say.

Then Mull thought of something good to say, so he said it.

"Something about this business that smells," he told Black. "And it's not hydrocyanic acid."

Black turned slowly and looked at Mull. He wondered whether any human being had ever been so tired of another human being as he was tired of Detective Sergeant Mull.

"Did you read that somewhere, Mull?" he asked him, "or did you just make it up?"

Mull smiled happily. "No, sir, I just made…." His voice tailed off. Belatedly, he acknowledged high-grade police sarcasm.

Nonetheless, he soon came back with another line: "Just a suggestion, sir… shoot me down in flames if I'm wrong…."

Black had a sudden mental picture of himself at the controls of an anti-aircraft gun.

"Do you think," Mull continued, "that we should keep a close eye on this Harris bloke?"

"Do I what?"

Black's tone was so neutral, so bland, that Mull felt totally lost. "Er… well… not to close… but quite close… or rather just a slight… or perhaps very… I mean… sort of… something?"

"Really?"

At this, Mull knew that, although he had suggested practically every variety of action he could think of, he had still failed to say the right thing. He waited miserably to be put right.

Black drew himself up with a deep breath. "Sergeant Mull!" he said with cold intensity. "I want you to watch Harris *so* close that if he so much as *farts* I want to know about it."

Mull winced and blushed. Farting was a subject he never discussed. Not even with his wife.

Tony left the flat first. He took a quick look up and down the corridor. He rang for the lift. Then he turned and beckoned Arthur and Fiona out onto the landing.

Arthur pulled the door to behind him and moved cautiously towards the lift. Fiona, he thought, looked as nervous as he felt.

Then Tony was hissing angrily at him: "Now then! You find a back way out. Fiona and I will drive round into the side road and wait for you."

"Right." Good Old Tony, Arthur thought. Taking charge. Organizing things. Where would they be without him?

"Bye, darling…." He moved to kiss Fiona, but Tony got an arm in the way.

"No time for that," he snapped. "Get going!"

He was right, of course. Arthur contented himself with a little wave, and slipped quickly through the door that led to the emergency stairs.

When he'd gone, Fiona looked resentfully at Tony. She had wanted to kiss Arthur good-bye. Tony was getting a little too bossy, even if he was helping them. She remembered that he'd been Arthur's friend, not hers. And she wasn't too sure about this plan of his, either.

"These… acquaintances of yours," she said critically. "They sound like criminals."

"They are." Tony was almost scornful. "Who else can we go to?"

Murderers, criminals, detectives, sudden death—

Fiona could hardly believe it had all begun because she got a little depressed and left home for a day. Other women left their husbands for a day without the world falling to pieces. Good grief, if this sort of thing happened every time Elizabeth Taylor…. She left the thought unfinished, and sighed.

"I'm worried."

Tony turned to her quickly, and draped an arm around her. I'll protect you!" he cooed. Fiona felt his hand sliding down below her waist and jerked it away.

"Worried about *Arthur*," she told him, and got into the lift. With bad grace, Tony followed her.

At first Arthur made good progress down the emergency stairs. He found it quite exciting—he'd never used the stairs before, was hardly aware that they existed. He'd reached the level of the first floor when he heard voices.

They came from below him, on the bottom flight. Perhaps at the foot of the stairs. They were the heavy, bored, resentful voices of people performing some thankless routine task. People like policemen. Arthur paused, crouching by the door which led into the first-floor landing, and listened.

"That Nelson's a sod," said the first voice.

"Um," the second agreed.

"He's only been a sergeant two years, and he's got a car, a speedboat and his missus has got a black diamond fur coat."

Yes, definitely police. Arthur swore to himself, Tony had been right. He'd been sure that the police would cover every exit from the flats, and so they had. Tony said that from now on they would stick to Arthur like glue. The thought had brought Arthur some relief. Perhaps they'd get in the way the next time the odd job man launched an attack. But Tony was convinced that the only answer was to shake off the boys in blue, and put their trust instead in his doubtful acquaintances. He insisted that somehow Arthur had to get out of the flats without being seen.

But, Arthur reflected grimly, insisting wasn't quite the same thing as doing. With the police guarding the emergency stairs he was trapped. Unless he could come up with some brilliant idea.

To give himself somewhere to go, Arthur opened the door and went through onto the first-floor landing. And then he had his brilliant idea.

Facing him was the door of the flat occupied by American Angie.

As far as was possible, Fiona and Tony also wished to leave the flats without drawing undue attention to themselves. As it transpired, they left with two police constables, two ambulance men, Black, Mull and the awful caretaker.

The constables led the way, ostensibly clearing it. There followed the two ambulance men, with the body on a stretcher between them. Mull and Black came next. They kept their faces firmly to the fore, wearing expressions that were at the same time grave and optimistic—the true look of the professional crimebuster! It was a look which never faltered, even when, to their enormous surprise, some press photographers flashed cameras in their eyes.

Fiona and Tony came next. They kept their heads down, and when the police procession turned to the left, towards the ambulance, they peeled off to the right.

Neither Black nor Mull noticed them.

They sat in Tony's car, and watched as Mull rushed around the forecourt, directing ambulance men to the ambulance, and police constables to the police car, and then directing the ambulance out onto the road, and then the police car out onto the road, and then sprinting after the police car and stopping it and getting one of the constables to come back to stand guard, and then directing Inspector Black's car out onto the road, and sprinting after that and stopping it, and getting in, and then getting out with a red face and coming back to the flats and going into the entrance hall to stand guard.

Then Tony started the engine of the Citroen, and they slid around the corner to wait in the side street as arranged.

Arthur took a deep breath and rang Angie's doorbell.

She answered it almost immediately. She recognized him at once, and a rather cool look crossed her squashy little face.

"Oh," she said.

"Ah… hello… there." Arthur smiled politely.

"Hello," said Angie. Arthur reflected that if she'd been English she'd have used a few well-chosen words on him, and slammed the door in his face. Probably she wanted to do just that. But as a foreigner, even an American, she found herself in the natural one-down position of not quite knowing the local form. Perhaps, she probably thought, it was not that unusual for an Englishman to get a girl naked into bed, washed, warm and ready to go, and then to turn around and go home. At the very least, she was experiencing a certain doubt as to how to deal with his reappearance. He pressed home his advantage.

"Sorry about the other night… I was…."

Arthur made an unsteady wiggling motion with

his right hand. Angie seemed to understand. American, English or Tibetan, most women accept drunkenness as a reasonable excuse for an inadequate sexual performance.

"Yeah, you were," she said with emphasis. And then, mercifully, "Come in."

He followed her through to her sitting room. He tried to visualize the scene with her, in this room, just two nights previously. But it was like something he might have seen on television years ago. He couldn't recall it in any detail.

She turned and faced him, and now the beginnings of her grin were showing.

"I won't stay long," he said.

She shrugged, and the grin became fully developed. "Be hard to stay shorter than the last time. I'm just fixing some coffee. Sit down."

She walked away into the kitchen. She was in trousers again. Washed-out denim, this time. Arthur admired her bottom, and for a short moment he was tempted to stay. The odd job man and the police would never find him here. Neither would Fiona and Tony. He'd be safe from the lot of 'em. And if he could get her into that bedroom again, this time he'd stay. It was a delicious, guilty, self-indulgent thought, and after a brief wallow in it, he put it firmly aside. Instead he went to the balcony window, and tried it gently. It was locked, but the key was there, and it turned easily.

"Terrible what happened to the caretaker!" Angie's voice carried piercingly from the kitchen.

"Yes, isn't it!"

He opened the balcony door, stepped through it, and went quickly to the balcony rail. From this, a first-floor flat, the ground seemed amazingly near. He straddled the rail, climbed right over, and lowered himself until he hung by his hands. Then he let go, and landed quite softly, after a fall of about four feet, in a small patch of grass.

"Hey!"

He looked up. Angie was looking down at him from the balcony. There was an expression on her face that made him wonder if he had ruined her sexual self-confidence forever. There was no time now to reassure her. He jumped from the grass to the pavement, then ran lightly down the road, crossed over, and veered into the side street.

There was Tony's car. Two heads—Tony and Fiona. He tumbled in, and Tony took off with a roar.

Opposite the spot where Tony had parked stood a row of garages. Some of the doors were open, and these open doors gaped blackly out at the street. From within the dark depths of one came a throaty rumble. Then out into the sunlight, and up the street after the Citroen went the motorcycle combination.

Thirteen

In the late 1870s it was built as a slum and for a hundred years it has gone steadily downhill. But it still stands, somewhere down where the docks used to be—a short straight little street of brown brick and wired windows. Once the buildings were houses of a sort. Now they house only goods, which are always on their way from somewhere else to somewhere else, and every day anonymous men in small trucks load and unload packages of packaging, stacks of shelves, and big boxes of boxes. Standing halfway down one side of this sorry street, and sticking out like a fashion ring on a sore thumb, is the Pink Goat Club.

The Pink Goat Club is easily identified by a slightly off-centre neon sign that hangs above the door and reads:

"Th   ink   oat." There is another small sign which informs clients of the brand of beer sold within, and further signs on the pavement outside testify that the beer does not sit too well on some stomachs. The door is closed and has a peephole, which is unusable because a West Ham supporter sprayed it with paint and no one's got round to cleaning it off. Instead each caller who rings the bell is inspected through the open door by a doorman. The inspection is perfunctory. People who would not be welcome at the Pink Goat Club know better than to attend the Pink Goat Club.

It has not always been the Pink Goat Club. Before it received its present name it was the Flash Harry. Before that it was the Rubadub Club. Before that, Emile's. Before that, Casey's. Before that, the Frisco Disco. Before that, The Spot. Within living memory it has also been The Hot Room, The Eagle, The Commodore, The Palace, The Left Bank, Chez Andre, and the Excelsior Coffee Bar.

To avoid any confusion that might arise from such a galaxy of names, the title of the company that own the club is neatly engraved on a plate by the front door. It is Besthaven Ltd.

Before the club was owned by Besthaven Ltd it was owned by Fairhaven Ltd. Before that it was owned by Fairlife Ltd. Before that, by Lifehaven Ltd. Before that, by Prestview Entertainments Ltd. Before that, Good Fun Ltd. Before that, Goodhaven Ltd. In living memory it has also been owned by Havenlife, Ltd, Donmick Ltd, Kingdor Ltd, Donnart Ltd, Malnip Ltd, Dunlad Ltd, and Fabulous Fair-do Entertainment Corporation Ltd.

The man behind Besthaven Ltd—who was also the man behind every other company who have ever owned the premises as an entertainment centre—is Mr. Sandy McTyre, of Dunne Street. Mr. McTyre has a job in a factory that makes things like cycle clips. It doesn't pay very much, so for a tenner Mr. McTyre will put his name to anything, and frequently does. He has never been to the Pink Goat Club, and indeed he has no idea that, to a certain extent, he could be described as the owner.

Tony parked his Citroen about a hundred yards away from the Pink Goat. He couldn't park it any closer. The kerb was crowded, either with vans loading up racks of racks, or with big beautiful smooth long polished cars, all of which outclassed the Citroen by miles and did nothing to improve Tony's temper.

He led the way up the pavement. Arthur and Fiona followed, close behind and holding hands. Arthur didn't like the look of it at all. He'd never seen quite such a dingy street in his life,, and he didn't understand why Tony was taking them to a night club when it was still the middle of the day. Surely no one would be there. The pavement was uneven and pock-marked with gratings, and Fiona, in her heels, had to keep stepping into the road and walking around cars. Arthur began to feel he'd prefer to return to the police station and throw himself on Black's mercy. But the prospect of telling Tony, after they'd come so far, was too intimidating. So, in the grim hope that whatever happened wouldn't be *too* disastrous, he stumbled on.

Tony stopped at the club door and rang the bell. Arthur put his arm around Fiona and gave her a comforting squeeze. Tony frowned at him. Displays of emotion were, it seemed, out of place at the Pink Goat.

The door was opened by a waistcoat. At least, that was Arthur's initial impression. Then, looking again, he realized it had been opened by a very very big man indeed. The waistcoat stretched to the door width. Massive pillars, clad in the same light check material, plunged groundwards like the legs of some gigantic oil drilling rig. The jacket hung impeccably on shoulders that disappeared on either side of the door frame. To walk through the door, the man would have to turn sideways. His neck was equally massive, and around it clung a whiter-than-white shirt, adorned with a tie featuring the smallest knot that Arthur had ever seen. Or did it just look small? Arthur realized, with a sense of admiration, that every stitch the man wore, apart from the tie, had been made to measure.

The head, therefore, was something of an anti-climax. It was not made to measure at all. It was definitely just a head off the hook. It was smallish and round, and rather unimpressive. Almost kindly. Perhaps to give it some character, the man had shaved his skull, but the desired effect of Slavic villainy was rather spoiled by half a cigarette behind the left ear. Arthur wondered at the financial approach which encompasses made-to-measure suiting and half-cigarettes.

The big man looked at them. Arthur tensed himself for a blast of sullen negative gang-land invective.

"Ello, then!" said the man, brightly.

Tony, with a certain diffidence that wasn't him at all, replied, "Hello, Boston," and led the way in as the man backed away down the corridor.

Arthur and Fiona found themselves in a small reception area. To one side was a small cloakroom, with a counter, and behind it a girl of quite staggering beauty chewed a little fingernail. A fire extinguisher hung on one wall, next to a large grainy photograph of Marilyn Monroe. A long velvet-and-gilt couch lined the other wall. It sagged slightly at one end, where a small bottle crate substituted for a missing leg.

The man called Boston checked that they'd shut the door behind them, then turned to Tony.

"Yeah?"

Was there the slightest quaver in Tony's voice. "Would you mind informing the Mr. Bennets that Mr. Sloane, a gentleman and a lady are here to see them?"

The man nodded, and picked up a phone on the reception desk. It was, Arthur noted, a modern "trimphone"—but badly cracked, and held together with Sellotape.

"Ello?" said Boston into the phone. "The Sloane Ranger is down here with a geezer and a tart."

Arthur loved the "Sloane Ranger." It was the kind of crack that usually would cause the lawyer to turn on the full strength of his courtroom scorn. The result, Arthur felt, might be fun to watch.

Tony's face twitched slightly. But he said nothing.

Boston put down the phone. "Right," he told them. "Follow me."

He led the way through a set of red curtains, and they found themselves in what had to be the main club bar. Arthur was amazed—the place was packed. Bodies pushed around the bar, sat at tables, worked pinball machines. Smoke filled the air, and the music of—yes, Arthur identified it—an early Neil Sedaka hit jangled from the juke box. It was as if the time was midnight, not whatever-it-was in the afternoon.

Boston marched, Moses-like, into the crowd, and obediently it parted before him. In single file, Tony, Fiona and Arthur followed through. Arthur had fleeting glimpses of quiffed hair-dos, lipstick black in the strange light, a jacket pocket edged with the clips of at least six fountain pens. Then they went through another set of curtains, and into a short corridor.

Annoyingly, Arthur found that he needed to pee. Nerves, he supposed. He touched Tony on the shoulder, meaning to ask him if he knew where the Gents was.

Tony turned, but spoke first, quickly and quietly: "What a man, eh?"

"Eh?"

"Boston." Tony kept it down to a whisper, pointing at the broad back in front of him. "The Boston Startler, as he's known. Was a great wrestler, you know. Until he killed someone in a bout."

"An accident?" Arthur asked hopefully.

"No." Tony looked as if the question had been quite unnecessary.

Boston stood to one side, as much as he could. "In there," he said, pointing at a door. Half this door was a panel of frosted glass, with the word "Office" painted on it. The glass was cracked, and had been repaired with a long strip of sticky brown paper.

They pushed their way past the Boston Startler—quite a feat in itself for Fiona, who somehow reduced a normal thirty-six-inch bust measurement to about twenty inches, to avoid contact—and Tony knocked on the door. The Startler rumbled away.

The office door was opened by another remarkable figure. Arthur noticed the boots first. Motorcycle type, calf-length, zippered and buckled. Into them was tucked a pair of dark blue jeans, that were moulded to slim but short legs. The front of the jeans bore an exposed gold zip, which outlined and emphasized a massive pubic bulge. Cotton wool, Arthur guessed. Surely it couldn't be....

And then Arthur thought there was something he should check. He looked at the face. Yes, it was the face of a boy. Just.

It was a white little face, perhaps appearing paler than necessary as it contrasted with the black leather Nazi officer style cap and the two very deep-red thick lips. It could have been made up, too. Arthur wasn't sure. Blond curly hair showed beneath the cap, and an earring hung from one lobe.

The rest of the boy was leather-clad, even down to gloves, and adorned with chains, spikes, badges, necklets, and even two or three gaudy jewelled rings thrust down over the leather fingers.

He looked... the only word, Arthur decided, was "choice."

Arthur felt Fiona tense at his side, and feel for his hand. He gripped it reassuringly. Fiona always grew awkward in the presence of doubtful sexuality. Perhaps because she was so womanly herself. Arthur felt that, personally, he could accept this sort of thing in his stride. After all, one of the partners at the office was as bent as a corkscrew. The post boy went in terror of his virtue. The only thing to do was to take people as you find them, in your stride. Especially at a time like this. He wished Fiona felt the same. He suspected that at any moment she would ask him, in a stage whisper, if he thought the boy was "a bit funny."

Tony made this unnecessary. "Hello, Batch," he said warily.

"Batch" pursed his lips and kissed the air. "Hello, Drear," he lisped. And, standing aside, he ushered them into the office.

It was empty, and Arthur was glad. He needed the breathing space, just to take in what met his eye. Because after the tattiness, the general atmosphere of dilapidation and faded luxury which marked the rest of the club, this room was a soft, smooth, and extraordinary contrast.

The first thing Arthur noticed was the smell. It was a rich, dark, walnutty scent, it spoke of much-washed and oiled bodies, of fruity expensive tobaccos, of new clothes and shoes. It was the smell of men who spoiled themselves. It wasn't unpleasant, and Arthur took in a deep lungful as he looked around the room.

The style of furnishing was surprisingly old-fashioned. A three-piece chintz-covered suite dominated half the room. But it wasn't the chintz of the cottagey middle-class. This was the best chintz, and while it hummed with bad taste, it also glowed with quality. In a corner a massive colour television showed the BBC2 test card in silence. By its side, an equally colourful drinks cabinet seemed to be stocked with nothing but Pernod, Bacardi and Southern Comfort. At the far end of the room stood a long desk, built of dark wood and topped with impractical white leather. Two padded chairs stood behind it. Built-in cabinets, of what Arthur first took to be a superior oak veneer, but which he then realized were in fact the real thing, solid oak, ran along one wall, housing, he guessed, sound equipment. The cabinets were studded with gilt handles in the shape of a clenched fist. The carpet, thick and luxurious, was a brilliant yellow, and spotless.

The whole room gleamed like a new pin, and clashed like a bell.

But what caught Arthur's eye—and what left Fiona open-mouthed in amazement—were the pictures on the wall. They were a mixture of posters, photographs and portraits, the majority presented in the pin-up tradition, but no matter how hard Arthur looked, he couldn't see a single female.

Instead the impression was of acres of bronzed male flesh. Boxers hugged their heads in massive shoulders and threatened the photographer. Body builders pumped up muscles as big as mole hills. Wrestlers gleamed in the light of their glittering trunks. Pop stars posed in see-through shirts and see-through smiles. Swimmers stood by pools, poised on the wink. There were even a few of the type of photographs once known as "Art Studies." Arthur wondered which subject Art was studying. He thought he knew.

This masculine montage was relieved by one—just one—female picture. Arthur had first looked for one of Marlene Dietrich, or at least one of her pretending to be a man. There were none—although there was one picture of a man pretending to be Marlene Dietrich pretending to be a man. But the exception stood on the desk itself, in a Victorian silver frame. It was a close-up shot of an elderly woman, who looked like Margaret Rutherford in a filthy mood. And just in case anyone got the wrong idea about it—or thought it *was* Margaret Rutherford in a filthy mood—it was identified by a ball-point legent in the neat handwriting of the near-illiterate: "Our Mum. God bless her."

A door at the far end of the room opened. Arthur straightened up from examining the picture. Into the room came two men. And at once nothing was the same as it had been before. Arthur had heard of people "lighting up" a room when they entered it, but he had never seen it happen before. However, that's just what these two did.

The first of the men was the younger of the two. He was immaculately dressed. More than immaculate—he made the Boston Startler, for all his made-to-measuring, look scruffy. He was bronzed, and had big, fleshy, handsome features and a full head of hair that was carefully combed and glossed. Gold gleamed dully from his cuffs, his fingers and the clip on the dark blue tie. Yet, despite everything, there was an air of the rough about him. He was smooth, but sharp. Relaxed but aggressive.

Arthur felt that beneath a veneer of highly expensive civilization, an animal lurked. A tiger.

But if the first was a tiger, Arthur realized as he tried to control his rather fanciful and over-stimulated imagination, then the second of the two was a teddy bear. He too had the same flash clothes, the same carefully mopped, mown and manicured presence. Indeed, it was clear from one glance that the two were brothers. Yet there was something funny about this one. He might have come out of the same mould, but someone had forgotten to file off the overspill. His outline was blurred, and his movements lacked the cat-like qualities of his brother—an impression born out when, coming into the room, he stumbled over nothing, looked round angrily, and nearly walked into the desk.

The first man took no notice. Instead, with a broad smile splitting the heavy face, and revealing a fourth source of gold, he strode across the canary carpet, his hand stretched out in greeting.

"Tone!"

It was the grand welcome. The glad hand. The Big Hello. And it clearly came from a very important person to a not-quite-so-important person. A four star general to a three star. Stalin to Trotsky. Dan Archer to Phil Archer.

Tony seemed happy with it. He simpered at the two men.

"Raymonde!" he said. Somehow you could hear the terminal "E."

And then: "Bernaard!" Both "A's" were clearly audible.

Tony turned and waved a hand at Arthur and Fiona. "This is Arthur and Fiona Harris."

Raymonde smiled like a shark. "I'm Raymonde."

Bernaard bumbled forward. "I'm B... B... B...."

Arthur's smile froze. The man had an astonishing stutter. Arthur foresaw hours of embarrassment and misunderstanding—to say nothing of wasted time—stretching ahead.

Batch came to the rescue: "He's Bernaard."

The interruption was not resented. Rather the contrary. Bernaard gave the boy a grateful smile.

Raymonde spread generous hands. "Why don't we all sit down?"

The brothers took the chairs behind the desk. Fiona and Arthur the sofa. Tony sat in one of the armchairs. Batch put away the flick knife with which he'd been pretending to clean his nails, and went and stood behind the desk between the two brothers.

There was a pause. Arthur heard Fiona suck her breath in. He wondered what had shocked her. Then he saw, and gasped a little himself.

Raymonde, lolling back in his chair, had reached up and begun to fondle Batch's thigh. Batch stood proudly still, and grinned slightly at the visitors.

Arthur noticed that Tony was watching this too. He looked uncomfortable and shifted in his seat. Arthur did the same, for a different reason. He now urgently needed the loo. He was about to ask for it when Tony spoke.

"Look...." He seemed a little upset. "This is a rather urgent matter. Shall we get down to it?"

Batch picked up a slight double meaning, and raised an eyebrow at Tony. Tony squirmed again.

"What's the problem, Mr. Harris?" Raymonde asked expansively.

Watching Tony's reaction to Batch, Arthur wasn't sure if it was he who had the problem. However, he spoke up: "Er... there's a man after me."

"Lucky old you!" Batch's response was predictable, and he followed it up with a long laugh only quelled by a look from Raymonde.

"Go on," Raymonde told Arthur.

"Well... Tony said maybe I should get some protection, and mentioned you."

"Hmmmmmm...." Raymonde relinquished the thigh, rose to his feet, and began to pace up and down, thoughtfully. He took out a gold ball-point and tapped his teeth with it. He looked for all the world like an investment consultant about to pronounce on the advisability of gilt-edged stock as opposed to equities.

"Hmmmm.... Depends on who's after you," he said. "If it's CID or Special Branch—dead easy. If it's

Secret Intelligence Service, or Customs and Excise, not too bad. But…."

He rounded on Arthur. His face grew grave, his voice tightened, an imperious finger stabbed the air.

"But… if it's American Express—no way!"

The finger symbolically cut the throat.

Arthur shook his head. "No… it's just one man and he's trying to kill me."

Bernaard pursed his lips. He only had one word to say, and he coped.

"Why?"

He was pleased, and looked to Batch for approval. Raymonde looked to Arthur for an explanation. Fiona and Tony looked at floor and ceiling in embarrassment. Arthur just looked ashamed.

"I employed him… to kill me," he muttered.

Batch, Raymonde and Bernaard exchanged glances, and Arthur blushed. "I know it sounds stupid," he admitted.

Bernaard tumbled into speech: "It sounds fu… fu…."

Batch grinned, then decided to spare Fiona's feeling. "He agrees," he interpreted.

Raymonde sat down. Once again he was the competent businessman. "I think we'd better have some details about this bloke. What's his name?"

Here we go, thought Arthur. "I don't know," he said. Raymonde shrugged. "Doesn't matter, where's he live?"

"No idea."

Raymonde looked up at Arthur, checked from his expression that he'd heard right, then looked at Bernaard. His brother was equally baffled.

Raymonde tried again. "All right, where's he hang about?"

"I'm sorry..." Arthur spread his hands in despair. "I don't know anything about him."

Raymonde became almost speechless with frustration. "Well... well... well... well, what's he look like, then?"

In a small voice, Arthur said: "I only met him once. He was about...." and he gestured a height of approximately four feet six, and went on: "And he wore a beret and a long leather coat."

Raymonde gaped. He looked at Tony. He looked at his colleagues. Why me? his expression asked. Why should I be landed with a berk like this? What can I say to him? What can I do for him? Why wasn't he put down at birth?

"A beret and a leather coat?" He sighed like a steam train. "Well... thank Christ we're not in France."

Arthur squirmed. He needed that loo very badly now. But it didn't seem the right moment to ask.

The club doorbell rang. The Boston Startler put his copy of *Grapplers' Monthly* back on the counter, walked down the corridor, and opened the door.

A little man stood there. When seen from the Startler's height, he appeared to be about four feet six inches. He wore a beret and a leather coat.

He reminded the Startler of another little man he had known. Tiny Laurie, the wrestling referee, had just been under five feet, and thin as an angle-poise lamp—a good gimmick in a heavy weight contest. Poor Tiny had once refereed a contest between the Boston Startler and the Canadian Fat Man Hughes, and was never the same again. Boston and Fat Man had fought each other many times. They'd got the running-across-the-ring-and-bounding-off-the-ropes routine down to a fine art. They could do it in their sleep. Only on this occasion somehow they got it wrong, and instead of missing each other, like police display motorbikes, they collided. As the Fat Man said afterwards, they might have hurt each other quite badly, had they not been lucky enough to sandwich Tiny Laurie between them. As it was, the referee absorbed much of the power in the impact. A no-contest was declared, and the little official was carried back to the dressing room and revived. No bones were broken. But Tiny swore that he had lost his appeal as a tiny referee because from then on he was at least two inches taller.

"Odd jobs?" asked the odd job man.

The Startler returned from his reverie with a jerk. Odd jobs? Well, why not? "Hang on," he said, and went to telephone.

Back in the office, Tony began to feel his feet. He started to speculate on how the brothers might help Arthur.

"You could sneak him out of the country," he suggested.

"Oh, yeah!" Raymonde brightened. He opened a desk drawer and pulled out a thick file. Arthur could just read the tag on the front of the file. "Rapid Removals Inc.," it said.

"Let's see," said Raymonde, running his finger down a page. "Two weeks in Benidorm? Three thousand quid?"

Arthur blanched. "That's a bit steep," he protested.

"That includes meals," Bernaard began with unusual fluency, "and a new p... p... p...."

"Passport," said Batch.

"Villa with swimming pool," urged Raymonde. "All the booze you can drink."

Arthur crossed his legs. The loo....

"And all the...," Tony began enthusiastically, then glanced at Fiona and changed what he was going to say "All the other amenities."

Fiona didn't miss the implication. She shook her head firmly. "Arthur doesn't like Spain much," she told them "Got anything in Greece?"

Batch grinned. "Amsterdam is nice this time of year," he suggested.

Yes, thought Arthur. And I know what it's nice for, too I read about it in one of the Sundays. He shook his head "I'll have to think about it."

The phone buzzed. Raymonde answered it.

"Raymonde speaking. What?... naw... oh, hang on." He snapped his fingers. "I know! Let him have a look at that pinball machine."

He put the phone down and smiled at them. "Sorry about that. Right, where were we?"

"Nearly in Amsterdam," said Batch with a leer.

"Actually we don't seem to be getting anywhere," Fiona said pointedly. She turned to Tony. "I thought you said they were good."

Batch sprang to the defence of his employers. "They *are* good," he told Fiona. And then, encouraged by a nod from Raymonde, he added: "You know the Great Train Robbery?"

Arthur couldn't believe what he was about to hear. The Great Train Robbery.... Well, even the police admitted that they'd never found the original organizing genius behind the crime. Was it possible that here, in this seedy little club, sat the two brains who organized the coup and baffled the country's top investigators? Millions of pounds were never traced. Could they be salted away, here, waiting for... well, waiting for something? Perhaps the whole place was only a front for a massive criminal syndicate. Perhaps… he took another long look at Raymonde and Bernaard. Surely not. Not really. It couldn't be.…

Fiona clearly thought it could be. She leaned forward, eyes shining, and breathed, "The Great Train Robbery…."

"Yeah." Batch glanced at the two brothers. They managed to appear both proud and modest at the same time. He looked back at Fiona.

"Well," he said, "they did the catering on that."

Raymonde was only too eager to remember the details. "Yeah. We done twenty-two tournedos Rossini, ten Duck à l'Orange, eight pizzas, and they drank…."

The mere mention of liquid was enough for Arthur. He stood up. "Where's the Gents, please?"

Batch sniggered. "Out the door, turn left, then right, then follow your nose."

Bernaard was still reminiscing. "And nobody traced the c… c…."

"Catering," Batch provided.

"Back to us," Bernaard finished.

"Yeah," said Raymonde. "We still get a card every Christmas from… er… whatsisname…." He began rummaging in his desk.

"Burt Reynolds," Batch tried.

"*Bruce* Reynolds!" Raymonde continued the search. "Now where is it…?"

Arthur left them to it. He followed Batch's instructions, and found himself back in the crowded bar. Across, in the gloom, a sign gleamed. " ents" it said.

Pushing his way between arguers, dancers, drinkers and talkers, Arthur slowly made some progress towards it. He reflected that whenever one needed to pee in a hurry, the forces of heaven conspire to make it impractical, in not impossible. People got in his way, his coat caught on a chair, he nearly spilled a big man's drink, he even had to take a long detour around some fool of a mechanic, who was head and shoulders deep in a broken pinball machine.

The obstacles remained even when he stumbled into the large and busy Gents. Every single stall was occupied. Swearing to himself, Arthur scanned the cubicles. There were a couple of open doors there. Quickly he hurried into the end one, unzipped, and prepared for that exquisitely painful first moment of relief.

Before he could begin, a hand tapped him on the shoulder.

Fourteen

The Boston Startler cracked his knuckles. He wished he could hit somebody. He also wished he had never set eyes on the little man in the long leather coat and the beret, because that had started him thinking about Tiny Laurie, and about his days in the wrestling ring, and thinking about that was guaranteed to upset his bowels.

It also upset the Bennet brothers. They didn't like the Startler to read or talk or even think about wrestling. It turned him funny. Of course they employed him for his strength and his antagonism. When, as is inevitable in a club like the Pink Goat, a mêlée of some kind threatened, Boston had the deterrent factor of a long-range nuclear missile. But when Boston began thinking about wrestling, things got muddled in his mind. The missile went out of control, and innocent peaceful people suddenly became targets. Unless, of course, Boston's upset bowels took over first. It was said that, at times like this, you could find the Boston Startler either in the lavatory or at the other end of a very hard fist.

On this occasion the odd job man was not entirely to blame for Boston's slide into violent incontinence. He had already weakened that morning and bought himself a copy of *Grapplers' Monthly*. There had been a time when the little magazine featured Boston's fearsome features regularly. Six times he'd made the "Star Of The Month" slot. Six times! He used to cut out the pictures and the articles and put them in a scrapbook. Muriel would have the scrapbook now.

Muriel.... Another feature of the past. Thoughts

about Muriel were also bound to upset his equilibrium, digestive and mental.

The Boston Startler knew his failings. But you can't control what you think about. At least, he couldn't. He leaned against the reception counter and opened the wrestling magazine at random. A picture of a bright new young wrestling star stared back at him. The boy had an oriental look about him. Probably half-Chink, Boston decided. He was working under the name Johnny Karate. "Johnny Karate!" the caption ran. "He chops champs into chunks!"

The Startler put his hand below the level of the counter, so that the cloakroom girl wouldn't see, and then made vigorous V-signs at the photograph. Chops champs? He'd like to have ten minutes in the ring with this beardless wonder. He'd bounce his arse off.

Boston's bowels moaned gently. He shouldn't be thinking about it. Raymonde got so angry. And yet....

It was a sin and a shame, everyone agreed, that a man like the Startler was not in there right now, grappling with the best of 'em. After all, he was only fifty. In the wrestling game, that's still young.

Fifty. That meant it was thirty years since he started. Give or take a year or two. In the army he'd boxed, and won a bit, too, but he hadn't really liked it. It was too brutal and direct, and someone was always getting hurt. He became a wrestler soon after demob. He and some mates had gone to a funfair, at Swindon, and inside a tatty tent, for the price of a shilling, he'd seen his first bout. Ten minutes later he was *having* his first bout. That night when the show left town, he left with it.

He was not a fairground wrestler for long. The sport was getting organized. Young, good-looking, athletic performers like Boston were snapped up by the newly formed promotion syndicates. Boston soon found himself out of canvas tents and into corn halls and assembly rooms, outside which gaudy posters proclaimed him to be Dennis Boston, the teenage Greek god. He was twenty-four at the time.

Boston ran his hand over his shaven head while he remembered. Plenty of hair in those days. Dyed blond. Peroxide. Maybe that was why he'd lost it so suddenly later on. Well, it was nice while it lasted. The ring rats loved it. They'd scream for him in the fights, and then afterwards, round the back where the van was parked, they'd let him have them all ends up, as long as they could ruffle up his carefully combed and creamed hair.

Muriel told him once that it was his hair which first attracted her. But he didn't like her to say that because it made her sound like a ring rat, and she most definitely was not a ring rat. No way. When he'd been going out with her for three months, some wrestler had asked him in the middle of a fight how his little red-haired ring rat was, and he'd punched the bloke right on the nose and been given a public warning, which was very rare because Boston at the time was an archetypal hero.

But it had been worth it. Muriel was not a ring rat.

Boston's intestines rumbled, and the magazine crackled in his fists. The cloakroom girl looked up, apprehensively. She knew the signs. One way or another, Boston was going to blow. And he was no respecter of the female sex. Last time he's split a girl's lip.

But he smiled now, as he remembered how Muriel had been at first. So admiring. She had this funny thing about him winning. She used to sit in the front row, always, and shout, "Kill him, kill him!" as he tackled his opponents. And then when he won she used to rush up and congratulate him. She was genuinely pleased. Funny, that. Heroes have to win. Most of the time, anyway. Yet she still got excited. And she embarrassed him a bit by sneering at the good wrestlers who played "heavies" and lost with style.

Then, in 1958, the promotions people called him in and said that, at thirty, he was getting a little old to be a teenage Greek god. They had a plan for him to go to the continent—yes, yes, he could take Muriel—and fight there for a year, until the wrestling public in Britain had forgotten all about Dennis Boston, the teenage Greek god. Then he could return, and they would have a new identity all ready and waiting for him.

Boston agreed. Which is why, in early 1959, wrestling crowds began to thrill to a new mature star they'd never seen before. Igor Zachz—Hungarian Freedom Fighter!

The newly born Igor enjoyed his personality. If a few suspected the truth, what did it matter? The majority believed—and of all people, Muriel believed.

By then they had a house, and Boston thought that perhaps he could look forward to some peaceful domesticity, with a wife who stayed at home and looked after the kiddies. But there were no kiddies, because Muriel still wanted to come to the shows, and she'd still sit in the front row and shout, "Kill 'im!" when "Igor" met a baddie. And now, at shows, even at home, she took to calling him Igor.

However, the personality of Igor, the Hungarian Freedom Fighter, was counted out in April 1963, when a national Sunday paper ran a routine exposure of the pretences of wrestling, and, almost as a sideswipe, revealed that Zimba the African Chief was born in Walsall, that the nearest Anouk of the North had been to Greenland was Carlisle, and that Boston was… Boston.

The promoters took a deep breath, and then did it all over again.

In 1964 two new mystery stars began to appear, separately, on the wrestling circuits. They both wore masks and leotards. One wore all white, the other all black. They both always won. Always. The one in white beat villains, fairly, against all odds. The one in black beat heroes, by means of foul play, cheating, and general bad behaviour.

The wrestler in white was billed as "The Sainted Angel." His friends knew him as Joe King. Or, inevitably, Holy Joe. He became the most popular wrestler in Britain.

The wrestler in black was billed as "The Messenger of Death," and was possibly at that time the most hated man in Britain, excluding politicians. But his friends still called him Boston.

It was inevitable that one day the two would meet in the ring. It was, said the promoters, written in the stars. More important, it was written in their contracts. Meanwhile, the spurious rivalry was carefully fermented.

It was Boston's first experience of playing the villain, and it made a pleasant change to hand out the treatment he'd received over so many years. But while he enjoyed tying his opponents up in the ropes, or punching them craftily in the kidneys, or pulling their hair, or simply backing off and complaining to the referee, Muriel sat in her ringside seat in cold and disapproving silence. And after a bout she often wouldn't speak to him for hours. He tried to explain that foul play didn't really damage an opponent, who often regarded a date with the Messenger of Death as a chance to have a nice restful bout with not too much wrestling involved. But she refused to understand.

"You're a rotten swine!" she told him. "The Sainted Angel will get you!"

Boston could still recall the way her eyes flashed as she said it. He grabbed his stomach. The pains were starting. Woe betide anyone who walked through the door now.

The match between the Sainted Angel and the Messenger of Death was billed, predictably, as the Fight Of The Century. Excitement rose, and the venue was sold out. Good was to meet Evil, in open combat. The winner would unmask—and thereby humiliate—the loser.

On the night, Boston and Holy Joe wrestled to a climactic, furious, shocking, awe-inspiring, inflammatory, rabble-rousing draw. Afterwards they had a quiet drink together.

Two months later they did exactly the same thing all over again.

The promoters decided that, for the third meeting of the giants, there had to be a positive result. One or two of the less gullible fans were becoming restless. So they shrugged with the calm acceptance of men who know they've taken a con as far as it will go, and on 15 March, 1965, the Sainted Angel used his superior wrestling skills to defeat the wily fouls of the Messenger of Death. Boston was unmasked. Everyone went home happy.

Well, not quite everyone. Although he had expected defeat, indeed had participated in it, Boston went home in despair because he went home without Muriel. She had watched the fight from her usual front row seat, but her screams and shouts of "Kill him!" had this time been in support of the Sainted Angel. Afterwards there was a note for Boston. Muriel felt she could no longer live with such a wicked, cheating, vicious villain. So she'd packed in advance, and gone. Boston, who had only ever cheated in the cause of art, didn't understand.

With money in his pocket—and the seeds of his personal tragedy in his mind—he took up a long-standing invitation and went to Canada. There he teamed up with Fat Man Hughes, whom he knew from the man's English tours, and together they wrestled around North America as a tag team, one of the toughest on a very tough circuit. In 1969 Fat Man was in collision with a truck in Toronto. Both were a write-off. When Boston returned to England four years later, his old promoters did not fail him. They shaved off the remainder of his hair, gave him a pair of black gloves to remove publicly before each performance, and re-named him the Boston Startler. Boston used his extensive experience of ring-craft and crowd psychology, and was soon once again a topflight villain of the British grappling ring. His brutality drew the fans for miles around.

This should have been his last and lasting personality. An extended career beckoned to him. A comfortable income. And the satisfaction of continuing to be top-billing draw, as he had been throughout his career.

But... and as he thought about it all, Boston's bowels began to rebel in earnest... but much of the satisfaction had somehow gone. Things seemed stale, pointless and seedy. It was Muriel, of course. He knew that. He missed her, yet he despised his memories of her, and regretted the years spent with her. He became tormented by the past, miserable, sullen, even savage. Once he hurt a young wrestler so badly in the ring that later, in the dressing room, the other wrestlers turned on him and beat him. It didn't help. Life had gone bad for the Boston Startler, and he went bad with it.

So perhaps when the end of Boston's career came, it was not a great surprise to those who knew him. He was wrestling the latest American pin-up in a hall in Wales, and he looked down and thought he saw Muriel in the front row, as she'd always been, and once again she was urging, "Kill him! Kill him!" Boston did as he was told. He lost all control and killed his opponent.

He couldn't work after that. The law called it an accident, and the promoters, in private, called it good publicity, but there was no way, they said, that they could put him back in the ring. And in truth they did not want to. The big man scared them. After twenty-five years, they wanted to pay him off, get rid of him, never see him again.

Their fears were justified. Boston took his pay-off cheque. But he left behind a wrecked office, three bruised and bloodied men, and a terrified receptionist.

Boston's guts sent him a final warning. Muttering to the cloakroom girl to keep her eyes on things, he pushed through the curtains and headed for the toilets. The crowd of drinkers moved out of his way with respect. He was the feller who killed a man in the ring.

The odd job man abandoned his pinball machine as soon as he saw Arthur heading for the lavatory. Arthur walked with the air of a man who has but one thing on his mind, and the odd job man followed on his heels, confident that he would not be noticed.

He waited while Arthur surveyed the busy stalls, then smiled with satisfaction as he watched him go to the unoccupied cubicle at the end of the row. As Arthur disappeared into it, the little man ran to the adjacent cubicle and slipped in, closing the door behind him.

Safely inside, he fished in his coat pocket and produced a hand grenade. He gripped the pin beneath his teeth, and pulled and twisted and wrestled with the thing until it came away.

The hand that held down the handle on the miniature bomb now trembled with anticipation.

The Boston Startler had no time to waste. He hit the Gents like a tornado with dysentery.

He saw the half-open door of Arthur's cubicle and pulled it open. The feller he'd taken to see the Bennets stood there. Enough reason remained for Boston to know that if he hit the man, then there'd be an even longer delay before he could lower himself onto the cold plastic seat. So instead he tapped him heavily on the shoulder, and when he turned, took his arm and propelled him forcibly out of the cubicle and towards the stalls.

Arthur didn't care. He saw a stall had now become vacant, and ran for it.

The Boston Startler slammed the door of the cubicle shut. He ripped down his expensive made-to-measure trousers. He lowered his massive bulk to the seat. Rumblings, groans, sputters, hisses, creaks, all signified that at least one part of the Startler's compulsive needs was about to be satisfied. For the other… well, Boston thought with a smile, in a moment he'd find some customer with a face that didn't fit, and then he'd….

The odd job man slipped silently out of his own

cubicle. He bent and looked under the door of the next one. He saw feet enveloped in trousers. He placed the grenade on the floor, counted two, and gave it a sideways nudge with his foot so that it rolled up to its target. Then he ran.

The blast blew the door off the cubicle, and Boston went to the next world with relief on his face and violence in his heart.

In the rest of the Gents many things happened at once. The tiled floor rocked. The frosted windows blew out. Smoke filled the room and flames licked at the graffiti. Urination ceased totally. In three cases it did not begin again, voluntarily, for some weeks. However, on the credit side, a severe case of constipation in one of the cubicles was immediately and permanently cured. Two fragile young things in another cubicle disentangled with difficulty, and squeaked themselves hoarse with fright. Another cubicle occupant, who had until that moment been happily reading through a book which he'd just purchased at the bar from an importer of Swedish literature, bit right through his tongue. Naturally the effects on the plumbing of the place were catastrophic. Anyone calm enough to look up at the big ventillation unit set high in the wall over the Startler's cubicle would have seen that this time, it really had hit the fan.

Everything happened so quickly that Arthur hadn't even begun to pee. And now the desire to do so was obliterated by terror and shock.

Instead he turned, breathless, unzipped, practically hysterical, and ran slap bang into the odd job man.

Instinctively he gripped the short man for support. The odd job man held him in wonder. They gaped at each other. The odd job man spoke, but in the screaming, banging turmoil that the Gents had become, Arthur couldn't tell what he said. He seemed to be pointing at Arthur, then at the source of the explosion, shaking his head… and then, as the meaning of these gestures suddenly became brilliantly clear to Arthur, the man tore himself free and ran like a rabbit out of the place.

As he ran out, Raymonde and Bernaard ran in. Arthur grabbed Raymonde by the lapels of his priceless suit. He could still hardly speak.

"It," he gasped, "it was… him!"

The light of battle flared in Raymonde's eyes. "Where?"

"Leather coat—it was him!" Arthur stammered, pointing vaguely at the exit.

It was George Reddington's misfortune that he had chosen that day to wear the short leather jacket which his wife had bought him for Christmas. He was the perfect innocent bystander. Well… not that perfect. He'd told his boss he felt ill that afternoon, and he'd been telling the blonde he'd just met that he was divorced. But he hadn't been anywhere near the Gents when the explosion had occurred, and had only just got to his feet in the bar to see what all the noise was about when two huge goons in sharp suits came rushing out of the loo and collared him and held him up against the wall and seemed all set to take him apart.

Arthur arrived just in time. "That's not him!" he screamed, looking wildly around the club. "He's gone!"

Bernaard and Raymonde relinquished their grip on George Reddington, and he fell into a little leather-jacketed heap on the floor. After a moment, Bernaard picked him up and dusted him down.

"I'm s… s… s…,"he began.

"He's sorry," Arthur interpreted, automatically.

Possibly George Reddington might at that stage have begun to complain, but his blonde friend thoughtfully took his arm and led him away. Having just found the man of her dreams—a divorcee who could afford a leather coat—she didn't want to lose him.

A distressed Fiona arrived, her arm in the possessive grip of Tony. She flung herself at Arthur, and he hugged her with relief, with fear, and with love.

"Oh, Arthur!" She was half-crying, half-laughing, so glad to see him. Then she said with suspicion: "Was it…?"

Arthur nodded dismally, and Fiona sighed.

Batch came back from a tour of inspection. "The Gents cottage is in a shambles," he announced. "And…" there was a break in his voice, "… the Boston Startler has finally lost a match."

"He's dead?" Tony queried.

Batch nodded.

Tony immediately displayed a generous measure of warm concern for himself.

"What? Look… a murder! I can't be seen here! It would be terrible! I've got to get out! Now!"

Raymonde took charge. "You scarper, Tony," he ordered. "And take the lady. *You,*" he said, turning to Arthur, "stay with us."

Arthur accepted the situation. He hugged Fiona. Tony pulled irritably at her arm. "Come on," he urged. "Come *on*."

Outside the club, he ran her down the road to the sound of approaching sirens. At the car, he fumbled with the keys, dived into the driving seat, and ducked down low as police cars, ambulance and fire engines swept past.

Fiona, left alone and exposed at the locked passenger door, stared in at him with contempt. She was heartened to see that, when he straightened up, he caught his head a nasty bang on the window winder.

Fifteen

Raymonde and Bernaard sat back in their chairs behind the long white-topped desk. Arthur hauled one of the chintz armchairs over to the desk, so that he could lean on it too. They all drank deeply.

Arthur's glass contained about three normal measures of Southern Comfort. He'd chosen this from the brothers' limited range of booze, because, of the other two choices available, Pernod tended to make him sick, and Bacardi made him randy, and quite frankly Arthur saw not the slightest chance of sexual fulfilment in either the near or the intermediate future.

Raymonde and Bernaard both drank a mixture of Pernod and orange juice, and furrowed their brows in concentrated thought. Arthur tried not to think. Everything that flashed into his mind now seemed like trouble. The odd job man still ranged free. Police help was now even more impossible. Another man was dead. And he didn't even have the comfort of Fiona by his side. Just these two strange men, with their suits and their funny little ways.

He drank again. The sticky American liquor clung to his teeth. He wondered if he was drinking too much. Ever since the night Fiona left, he seemed to have been diving for the bottle. Perhaps he'd escape the odd job man only to die of cirrhosis of the liver. No, he told himself, in the grip of melancholia. No, that's not the way drunks die. Drunks die of hopelessness. Drunks die after years of pottering around bars near Leicester Square, asking anonymous barmen if Jack's been in, and then retrieving glasses in the hope of a free half. Arthur shivered, and tried to think of something else.

Wasn't his present situation sufficiently horrendous, without imagining another?

Raymonde drained his glass and came to a decision: "Better forget about Benidorm. This nutter'll find you wherever you are."

Tell me something new, thought Arthur.

Raymonde got to his feet. "We'll look after you," he said with confidence.

"Two of you?" Arthur was sceptical.

"Course not." Again Raymonde spread those large generous hands. "We'll have fifty men protecting you."

Bernaard looked up, puzzled. "But we haven't got f… f…."

Raymonde glossed over the objection with serpentine smoothness. "Of course we haven't. It's nearer sixty." Then, as a direct order to Arthur: "You stay here till we get rid of the law."

Arthur didn't object. His bladder problem, which the blast had postponed, had been satisfied in the brothers' private loo—a lavender palace of glistening chrome knobs, surprise douches, and drawers full of exotic rubber appliances. Fiona was safe with his best friend. The odd job man was, for the time being, frightened off. He poured himself another Southern Comfort. In a familiar, alcoholic way, he felt safe.

Once in the corridor outside the office, Bernaard rounded on Raymonde so quickly, he nearly sprained his ankle.

"What was all that about s… s… s… s…"

Raymonde listened with affection as his brother wrestled with the gift of speech. Bernaard was really his soft spot. As a gang-land leader, Raymonde was a tough, brutal man. Only his brother, his one-and-only big brother, could pierce the tough exterior of the racketeer, and reach the tender, sentimental, caring man inside.

At least, that's what his publicity hand-out would say. If he ever got round to it. It might help people to understand that it wasn't their fault that he and Bernaard were crooks. It was society's fault. Course it was.

And his father. It was definitely his fault too. Perhaps if Mr. Bennet Senior had been content to remain a poor out-of-work docker all his life, then maybe the brothers would have stood a chance. But oh no, his father couldn't even do that for his sons. He had to become an out-of-work charge hand, and move out to Chingford.

That's where the boys were forced to mature, in the lawn-mowing, lager-drinking, car-washing streets, the acknowledged brats of a couple who were not only married but, what was worse, to each other.

The house they lived in was a disgrace. With four bedrooms, he and Bernaard had their own rooms, even when people came to stay. What chance did a boy have of developing a real background from which to rise, if he never slept three-in-a-bed, including the bed-wetter?

School was worse. The complete absence of physical violence scarred Raymonde's soul from his first day. At break he couldn't find a single boy to hit. Teachers who really cared talked to him about trust and confidence. Raymonde tried to shrug it all off, but the frustrations built up and up. Comparative religious studies were the last straw.

When he left school at eighteen, with nine "O" levels, three "A" levels, and a charity scholarship, Raymonde faced a bleak future. Only university, industry, commerce or the professions would touch him. Bitterly, he faced his father with the ultimate savage indictment:

"If it hadn't been for you, I might have been Michael Caine!"

So it was, perhaps, fate which caused his mother to throw an electric fire into his dad's bath one night, and take the family back east again. Raymonde fulfilled his destiny. Eventually he assumed responsibility for all crime in the East End. And, automatically, he also assumed responsibility for his big brother.

Raymonde patted Bernaard's arm. "That was just to keep him happy."

"How are we goin' to protect him?" Bernaard asked in a rush.

"We're not," Raymonde said succinctly. "We'll use Harris as a decoy, to get the bloke what done in our dear departed mate."

He winked at Bernaard, and led the way into the bar.

Detective Inspector Black was there already. He'd left his car in the street, and been swept in, alone, on a tide of firemen and ambulance drivers—the same ambulance team, he noted, which had attended the flats that morning.

He felt doubly relieved to be on his own. First, because Mull was not with him. It was like suddenly not having toothache, or not needing "L" plates any more. It was like the death of a grumpy and demanding old relative. A negative pleasure, but a pleasure nonetheless. The second reason he was glad to be on his own was that now he could more easily merge into the background. Black was sure that, if he could enter the Pink Goat unnoticed and proceed to detect undetected, then he stood a very good chance of getting to the root of the problem right away. So he pulled his hat over his eyes, turned up his collar, and sneaked in behind a fat fireman.

Batch spotted him in an instant. "Ooooh!" he whooped. "All these uniforms! Hello, Blackie! How's Vera?"

Black turned a jaundiced eye on the boy: "Isn't it about time you got a motorbike to go with that outfit?"

Batch squirmed with pleasure. "Oh!" he breathed, with synthetic passion. "I love you when you're dominant."

Raymonde slid smoothly through the curtains and up to the pair. "Hello, Blackie," he said with spurious friendship.

"Hello, Bernaard," Black replied blandly.

Bernaard fell for it. Indignantly he began: "I'm B…b… b…."

Black let him blow for a while. Then, when he'd had enough, he smiled in agreement. "So you are," he said.

"How's Vera?" Raymonde put in smoothly.

"She's fine. Now, what *is* all this…?" But Black had to stop. Something had gone wrong already. He thought back. Yes. "Listen," he objected, "My wife's name is Margaret."

Raymonde struck his forehead with exaggerated regret. "So it is. Sorry." And then, slyly, "Who's Vera, then?"

Black counted to ten, then continued: "Let's have a statement."

Raymonde gestured towards the still-smoking Gents. "Got a lot of clearing up to do, Blackie. Tell you what—we'll put one in the post."

Black drew himself up, and gave it to Raymonde, straight, cool and authoritative. "I want one now!"

"Fair enough." Raymonde gave him the big smile

of the co-operative citizen. "I'm busy, but my brother knows all the facts." And he slid away.

Bernaard was only too happy to oblige. "Well, we was s… s… s… sitting… i… in the o… o… o… o… o…." Black sighed, folded his notebook away, and went to look at the damage.

This time the odd job man went by bus. He'd decided that the old combination was becoming a bit of a giveaway.

Whistling, he strolled into the flats, past the empty caretaker's cubby hole, found the lift waiting for him, and rode straight up to Arthur's floor. In his hand he carried a brown canvas tool bag, which clinked when he joggled it. He unlocked Arthur's door with Arthur's key and went inside. All was quiet and deserted.

The odd job man smiled. This time, at least, things were going to plan.

He pattered through the sitting room and out onto the balcony. He dumped his tool kit down on one of the metal chairs, opened it, and selected a short dumpy saw. Then he took a good long look at the balcony rail. It was of thick, seasoned wood, very sturdy, and painted white. The odd job man reckoned he'd go through it like a knife through butter.

He chose a section in the centre of the rail, directly opposite the sitting room doors. He began the right-hand cut just to the left of a metal stanchion. He sawed steadily n short rhythmic strokes, and as he worked he hummed a rather basic version of "In the Mood," to the same rhythm. *Doo*-dee-*doo*-dee-*doo*-dee-*doo*-dee…

In a few minutes he had sawn almost through the rail, de stopped, and worked the saw free. To make the left-hand cut, he chose a spot about a yard and a half along, just to the right of the next stanchion. It took no longer to saw through. *Doo*-dee-*doo*-dee-*doo*....

He had almost finished the second cut, which would have left the section of rail neatly severed at both ends, when a car arrived in the forecourt below him. It was a Citroen. He noticed it because of the squeal of tyres as it turned in, the further screech as it braked violently, and the clatter as it knocked over a bicycle. As he looked, the passenger door opened, and he recognized the blonde bobbed hair of the woman who appeared. It was the wife! Mrs. Harris! The wife of his target!

The odd job man skittered away from the balcony edge. So they were back. They'd been quick. This could mean trouble. He turned quickly and began to pack away his tools.

Coming up in the lift, Tony didn't say a word. He used the silent technique. He stood close to Fiona and gazed into her eyes. You are mine, and I am yours, his eyes told hers. Together. Just us two. And something very wonderful will happen when....

Fiona spoiled the message by looking away.

He opened the flat door for her, and stood aside to let her in first, with a courtly bow. He followed her, closed the door and fastened the chain, then turned, arms wide to enfold her within them.

She wasn't there. She'd walked briskly into the sitting room, and from there to the kitchen, where she was checking for intruders. Tony positioned himself in the sitting room so that when she strode back through the door she almost walked into him.

Tony put his hands tenderly on her arms. "Fiona," he said in a husky whisper.

"What?" She hadn't heard.

"Fiona!"

"Well? What?"

"Fiona! Relax!"

"You can relax if you want to. I'm going to check the other rooms." She walked around him and set off for the bedroom. Then she turned. "If you want to make yourself useful, Tony, you can check there's no one on the balcony."

Tony clicked his tongue in annoyance. Very well. He could wait. He strode to the balcony, fumbled with the key, then realized that the balcony doors were not locked Sniffling at such a lack of security, he opened them.

The odd job man knew the couple had entered the flat when he heard the door bang. He flattened himself against the wall by the doors. It occurred to him that if Harris came out onto the balcony he could easily just tip him over. Then he abandoned the plan. Too public—and his wife would see it.

He heard more doors and vague voices. He realized, with a shock, that they would be checking to see if he was in the flat. That meant in any moment they would check the balcony. He looked around quickly. There was only one thing for it.

He moved to the side of the balcony and climbed over the rail. Then he gently lowered himself until he was clinging by his hands to the bottom of one of the support stanchions His whole body swung below the level of the balcony. He'd hardly hung for a moment when the doors above opened and he heard the footsteps of his target walk out onto the balcony.

He tensed as the footsteps approached the point where he had sawn the rail. There was a pause. Perhaps almost ab audible creak. Then the steps turned and walked back inside the flat, closing the doors behind them.

Arms aching, the odd job man slowly pulled himself up and over the balcony rail. Listening, he became aware that the dull rumble of a man and a woman's voices had begun again.

Tony backed Fiona around the sitting room: "Fiona!"

"What is it now?"

"Come on now, Fiona. Come on."

"Come on? I'm not coming anywhere. I'm staying here to wait for Arthur."

"You know what I mean, sweetie."

"I do not know what you mean. Sweetie."

"I mean, well, look, haven't I done a lot for you, eh? Don't I deserve a little reward?"

"You'll have to wait."

"Oh. You mean, you're on."

"I mean, Arthur's got the cheque book. No doubt he'll write you out a handsome little reward when he's safe and sound."

"Fiona, I don't want money. I want you. Fiona—I love you very much indeed."

"And I love Arthur."

"Yes, but you do like me a little bit, don't you?"

"No."

"Fiona! You're a tease, that's what you are. A naughty little tease."

"And you, Tony, are a pain in the arse."

"Oh, yes. Talking of arses, I've wanted to do this for a long time."

By now Tony had backed Fiona up to the side of the sofa. He put his arms around her, then quickly slid his hands down, cupped her buttocks, and squeezed.

Fiona stamped her heel on his Hush Puppy.

Hopping and swearing, Tony wagged a furious finger at her. "Now look here, love, you're getting a bit too precious for your own good, you are! Just who the hell do you think you're playing around with, eh? Listen, I've put myself on the line for you. You come to my flat when you're in a mess. Accept my hospitality. You drank enough vodka that night, you know. And when you ring me up and expect me to drop everything just because that stupid little twit of a husband of yours has dropped himself in the shit. But do I complain? No, I just fix you up with two of the best crooks in town *and* I nearly get mixed up with a murder at the same time. And now, when I've done all this for you, you're too bloody precious to give me a quick screw. Well, you better just change your mind, sweetie, or you're going to regret it, and quick."

He paused. Fiona looked back and said nothing.

"Well, all right, love." Tony gingerly rested his foot on the floor. "No more recriminations. You know where we stand. You just play your part, there's a good girl. Go on in the bedroom, and get your things off. I'll be there in a minute. We'll have some fun. You'll enjoy it. You'll see."

Fiona turned and walked into the bedroom. She returned almost immediately. She had the Samurai sword in her hand.

"Tony!" she said. "Get out now, or I'll cut it off."

Tony said "Shit," and left.

The odd job man couldn't hear a word of the conversation. But shouting, and a banging door, told him his target had had a row with his wife.

He risked a look in, and saw that the wife had been left alone. She was carrying a bottle and a glass, and walking into the kitchen. The target had left.

He turned the latch on the balcony doors, and

slipped soundlessly into the sitting room. He tiptoed across the room. In the kitchen he could see the wife's back. She was hacking viciously at an ice-tray with a pointed knife. He sprinted into the hall, then quietly opened the main door.

He was almost too late to see his target. The man was just getting into the lift. The odd job man saw one leg and the back of his jacket.

Then the odd job man moved with the speed of a whippet. He dashed up the corridor, and plunged down the steps to the next landing, flinging out a hand to jam against the lift "down" button. The lift pinged! He'd caught it!

Without pausing, he dashed on down another flight, and did the same. And again and again, at every landing down to the ground floor, he pressed the "down" button. Then he ran on out into the sunshine.

Tony thought the lift must have been made by a communist. He was not dissuaded from this opinion even when he saw that the manufacturer's address was in Northampton. The damn thing insisted on stopping at every bloody floor, even though there wasn't a soul waiting. It was ridiculous. It was just another example of how bloody inefficient everything was these days. Angrily he kicked the aluminium side of the lift. He felt that it wasn't his day.

Eventually, an age later, the lift opened at the ground floor. Tony strode out. He thought of having a bitter word with the caretaker. Then he remembered that the caretaker was dead. Well, that was no excuse for inefficiency. He'd write to the landlords.

He walked briskly across the forecourt, opened the Citroen, and sank into the driving seat with a sigh of relief. He sat still for a moment, remembering the feel of Fiona's bottom. The cow! He jerked the engine into life, reversed violently, and shot out, horn blaring, into the traffic. A violet Cadillac hooted back. Tony ignored it.

Huddling down behind the front seats of the Citroen, his face buried in an old rug to mask any pale reflection, the odd job man flexed his fingers.

The violet Cadillac turned into the forecourt with the slow speed and immaculate precision of a presidential limousine in a formal parade. It stopped in front of the main entrance, doors opened, and Raymonde and Bernaard slunk out like secret service agents, stalking around the car in a threatening manner until they were sure that all was clear.

Then, at a nod, Arthur emerged from the back seat of the Cadillac, and all three men shot into the entrance hall.

Raymonde and Arthur waited for the lift. Raymonde sent Bernaard to check the emergency stairs, and he reappeared out of breath but happy.

"It's all cl… cl… cl… cl…." he tried.

"Clear, is it?" Raymonde asked. "Good."

"Ye… ye… ye…." Bernaard began, then gave it up and nodded.

The lift pinged its imminent arrival. After a moment's thought, Raymonde shoved Arthur behind him, and the brothers waited to see what or who the doors might reveal.

It was Mr. Kemp and his corgi. Walkies time again.

Raymonde and Bernaard crowded him. Mr. Kemp wondered why on earth two such big nicely dressed men should display such a flattering interest in him. Then he saw Arthur peeping nervously from behind them, and his heart sank. He realized then that something disastrous was about to happen, and he composed himself for death.

"This him?" asked Raymonde.

"Oh, no." Arthur shook his head violently. "No, no."

Raymonde and Bernaard stepped solemnly back, and ushered Mr. Kemp out of the lift. Mr. Kemp realized he had been reprieved. Life was sweet.

"Good evening," he wished them.

"G… g… g… g "

"Good evening," said Arthur. And the three of them entered the lift.

At Arthur's floor there was cause for genuine alarm. The flat door was open. Arthur felt a new fear clutch at his stomach. Perhaps the stunted little bastard had got at Fiona.

Raymonde waved him to stay where he was. Then, like two avenging sharks, he and Bernaard charged through the open door, and disappeared. There was a brief silence—then a shrill scream and a crash.

Arthur lost all fear. He barrelled through the hall and into the sitting room and collided with Bernaard. Fiona stood by her chair. A broken glass lay at her feet, and her dress was splashed. Her face had the look of a driver who's just been missed by a juggernaut.

"It's all right, darling," Arthur told her. "It's only us." And she fell into his arms with a faint cry.

Tony's raging fury lasted for about ten minutes. Then, as he drove on, his lawyer's brain took over, and he planned a course of action.

First, he would call off the protection. He would cancel Raymonde and Bernaard. That would teach his so-called friends to take his for granted. Then he would inform the police of the situation. That, after all, was his duty both as a citizen and as a member of the legal profession. Arthur, if he lived long enough, would be arrested. The charge, he thought, would be aiding and abetting murder. Then Arthur would really need him. And Fiona....

He switched on the car radio. He didn't listen to it, but considered it an indication of status. He wound down one window, so that pedestrians at traffic lights would hear it. Radio Four, of course. Thinking man's radio.

The odd job man was grateful for the radio. He hated to miss the Archers. He was concerned about Tony's relationship with Pat. He waited until it was over, and then, as the car slowed, he carefully poked his head up and looked through the side window.

The car was facing down a steep incline, and coming to rest at some red traffic lights at a major road. It was the only car in sight.

Perfect!

The odd job man knelt up, and neatly strangled Tony to death.

It was only when the head fell back, and the dead features were reflected in the driving mirror, that the odd job man realized the driver was not his target.

"Bugger!" He climbed wearily out of the car and looked up and down the road. Still no one around. He opened Tony's door, made sure the gear lever was in neutral, then released the handbrake. He slammed the door, turned, and walked calmly up the hill. The car moved silently away down the slope...

The crash was long, loud and fearful. But the odd job man didn't bother to look.

Raymonde organized the sleeping arrangements:

"You two in the bedroom as per normal. Me and Bernaard will be out here. One of us will sleep on the couch, while the other keeps guard. Four hours each, turn and turn about. There'll always be one of us awake."

"Great!" Arthur enthused.

"We're so grateful to you," Fiona added.

"Yeah, well…." Raymonde wasn't accustomed to gratitude. He blushed beneath his tan. "Sorry to have to say this, but will you please go to the toilet before you go to bed. I don't want you getting up in the middle of the night."

"Quite…." Arthur turned to Fiona. "After you, darling. Well, goodnight all."

"Night," said Raymonde.

"S… s… s… s…." Bernaard began. They waited.

"Sweet dreams?" Raymonde suggested.

"S… s… s… s…."

"Sleep well?"

"S… s… s… s…."

"Stop worrying?"

"S… s… s… s…."

Raymonde shrugged helplessly. Arthur and Fiona nodded in embarrassment, and left the room.

Bernaard turned sadly to his brother. "I was going to say 'See you tomorrow.'"

Black was at his desk, making out his report, when Mull knocked on his door. He knew it was Mull, partly because the detective sergeant had invented his own complicated code knock, and partly because he could never remember that the door opened outwards, not inwards, and therefore spent several seconds struggling with it before realizing his mistake, tugging the thing open, and stumbling into the office. Black sighed, and kept his eyes on the desk.

Mull decided to start with an apology. The essential thing about being a good detective sergeant is to know when to apologize to the detective inspector.

"Sorry I'm late, sir."

"Are you?"

"I had to wait for the relief watch. I couldn't leave Jenkins there on his own."

Black looked up at him for the first time, and thought how he loathed the man. "Is there any point in having Jenkins there at all?" he asked.

Mull blinked. "We have to cover each exit, sir."

"Cover? Cover?" Rage swelled inside Black. His shoulders bulged, his face flushed, and he slammed a fist down on the desk. There was a long silence.

Then there was fatigue and resignation in Black's voice: "Give me your handkerchief, Mull."

"Sir?"

"Hand—ker—chief!"

Mull produced the immaculate white linen handkerchief which his wife ironed so carefully for him every Sunday evening. Black took it, wordlessly. Then slowly he lifted the hand which had slammed onto the desk. Beneath it his fountain-pen lay in three pieces. Ink flooded his report, his blotter, and other forms. Black used his other hand to scrape up all the stained paper and throw it in the waste bin, protecting his hand with Mull's handkerchief. The shattered pen followed the paper. Then, his eyes on Mull's face, he used the handkerchief to scrub at the ink on his other hand, until the worst was gone. Then he threw the handkerchief deliberately into the bin.

Mull decided not to say anything.

"So you had both exits covered?" Black asked him in a normal voice.

Mull nodded. "Yes, sir. There was no way he could have got out."

"I see. So we just have to account for him coming back in."

Mull writhed in his misery. He still couldn't accept that Harris had left the flats without being spotted. "Yes, sir," he muttered.

Black wasn't about to let him off the hook. "So while you were keeping watch, Harris slips out, and then arrives back with the Brothers Gay, whose club, the Pink Goat, was the scene of another murder earlier this evening."

Mull looked at the floor. "It could be connected, sir."

"Oh, could it really?" Black was going for his PhD in Police Sarcasm. "Could it really? Well. Sergeant Mull, let me tell you something—and this isn't an order, Sergeant Mull, it is a prophecy."

"Yes, sir?"

"If Arthur Harris from London so much as grows a hair on his head without you giving me a four-page report on it, I'll have you arrested for aiding and abetting."

Sixteen

It was eight in the morning. Raymonde was on watch. He was asleep. His chair, one of the upright dining variety, leaned back against the bedroom door. Security! His chin rested on his chest. His dreams were of Batch, and very private.

Bernaard was off watch, and therefore slept the sleep of he just. He lay precariously on the sofa, his knees projecting over the edge, and he snored with a stutter. "Z… z… z…."

The phone rang. Bernaard turned over restlessly and fell off the couch.

On hands and knees, he looked wildly round the room. Memory flooded back. He looked at Raymonde, noticed that he was asleep. The lazy b… b… b….

Still on all fours, Bernaard called to his brother: "R… R… R… R…." Daunted, but still hopeful, he tried another word. "T… t… t… tel… tel…."

He began to get up, and the phone stopped. At that instant Arthur, in a fog of sleep and knowing only that he had to answer the bloody phone, opened the bedroom door, inwards. Raymonde's chair tipped backwards and fell on the floor.

"Waaaa!" yelped Arthur. That woke everyone up. Raymonde sprang to his feet and took a swing at him. Bernaard waved a feeble speechless hand. Fiona sat up in bed and screamed.

Arthur was the first one to make sense: "Who answered the phone?"

Bernaard knew the answer: "St… st… stopped."

"Hell!" Arthur's fist hit the side of his pyjamaed thigh "It might've been *him*!"

Fiona wandered through, in her pale lace bathrobe, like some benign White Lady. "The answering machine," she said sleepily. "It's been used."

She knelt by the thing, and pushed buttons which none of the others, especially Arthur, felt capable of operating so soon after waking up. But they all gathered round and listened, as the recorded message began:

"Hello, Mr. Harris."

Oh, God! It was *him* all right. Arthur's mouth hung open as he listened to that piping, chirpy, ingratiating, humble deadly voice.

"This is your odd job man here. If I'd known it was going to be so hard to kill you, I'd have charged you more. I'll see you in Regent's Park Zoo, at eleven o'clock. That'll be a nice handy place for you to snuff it. Just walk around, look at the animals. I'll find you. Hope you are well. Good-bye for now."

Arthur looked at Fiona, horrified. Bernaard looked at Arthur, horrified. Fiona looked at both of them, horrified. Then all three looked at Raymonde, who grinned, winked and rubbed his hands with glee.

"That's it, mate. We're home and dry," he told Arthur.

Arthur lost all faith in the criminal classes. "What? He's going to kill me!"

"No no no." Raymonde shook an admonitory head. "Listen We all go off to the zoo. You wander round looking natural like. He's got to come out into the open to kill you, and then—we've got him!"

Bernaard nodded with great enthusiasm.

Fiona nodded with reasonable enthusiasm.

Arthur nodded with a marked lack of enthusiasm.

Detective Sergeant Mull spent the entire night in a Ford Escort van, reading the *Evening Standard* and watching the flats. He reflected that the *Evening Standard* was not designed for all-night reading. He first read the cartoons, the news, the articles and the sport. Then, like many a bored Londoner, he found that there was more in the thing than first met the eye. He read the recipe. He read the stars, he did as much of the crossword as was possible, he even tried to understand the bridge problem. He read the City page, the weather, the television preview, the small advertisements, the letters, the shopping column, he even, in desperation, read some dootling radio review.

Detective Sergeant Mull felt that his night had been a long one. He had really suffered in the cause of law and order. Mind you, it helped being a Conservative.

Black pulled up by him in his Cortina. Mull climbed out of the van, scattering a cloud of fluff, cigarette ash and car wax, and went over to the window.

"Morning, sir."

"Umph."

"No sign of them." Mull felt crisp and efficient. "They haven't moved."

"Umph." Black pointed a lazy hand through the wind-screen. "What's that, then?"

Mull followed his finger. From the front door of the flats a quartet of figures emerged. The Harris man, his wife, and the Bennet brothers. The wife was holding Harris's and hand talking fondly to him. They all climbed into the big violet Cadillac and drove away.

"Well?" Black asked irritably.

"Well...," Mull was at a loss.

"Well, get in, dummy!"

Mull hurried round to the passenger door and climbed in. he Cortina shot off in pursuit.

Raymonde found a meter near the zoo entrance and parked. Then he turned, leaned over the front seats, and talked to Arthur and Fiona:

"Right you two. So it's just a nice day out at the zoo, then. You two just relax. Walk a little bit in front of us. We'll do the work. Don't worry."

Don't worry, thought Arthur. Don't worry. You two Christians walk out into the arena, and if the lion come we'll scare him off for you. Don't worry. Slowly he and Fiona climbed out of the car. The summer breeze seemed cool. Sounds were unnaturally clear. He remembered how he'd felt when he'd entered the park just forty-eight hours ago. It felt like forty-eight years.

They walked up to the turnstiles, Raymonde and Bernaard just behind them. Raymonde eased forward with a five pound note, but Arthur waved him away.

"I'll get this."

"It's all right." Raymonde was used to paying for even body. "I'll do it."

"No, please," Arthur insisted. "It's the least I can do."

"Oh, well." Raymonde shrugged. "It's your funeral."

Arthur's look told him that he'd said the wrong thing. He grimaced. "Sorry."

Arthur turned to the ticket window. "Four adults, please."

Shortly after them came Black and Mull. Mull, in an attempt to get back in Black's good books, offered to pay. Black elbowed him off, flashed his warrant card, and went through. After a moment's hesitation, so did Mull.

Arthur felt like a sitting duck. He imagined himself as one c those little tin-duck-shaped targets that rattle round on wires at seedy fairground shooting stalls, waiting to be blasted by airgun pellets. Only in his case it wouldn't be airgun pellet it would be dum-dum bellets, or .303 slugs, or whatever. How could the odd job man miss a target like him, out there in the open at the zoo? What a simple shooting gallery! Bang, clang, give the man a plastic windmill.

Fiona tugged at his sleeve. Arthur nearly died.

"Don't do that!" he snapped.

"It's you," she told him. "You're making yourself far too obvious. Try and look natural when you walk."

Look natural. Did a condemned man look natural when he walked the last thirteen steps? Arthur did his best, but realized that his walk had taken on all the awkwardness of marionette. It wasn't a natural walk, it was a judder from side to side. He couldn't help it and he couldn't stop doing it. His left arm was swinging in time with his left leg, and vice versa. He tried to swing his arms normally, but when he did, he found he swung both arms forward together, and his legs stopped, and he nearly fell over. He resumed the arm-and-leg-together movement, remembering as he did so who his peculiar gait reminded him of. Of course! Muffin the mule!

The explosion was loud, close and frightening. Even though Arthur had expected it. He fell face first, off the path, onto the grass verge.

He had begun to think: so this is death… when in front of his nose crawled an insect of repulsive appearance, and he realized that this wasn't death at all, this was just lying on one's face in the park. Just as he had two days previously, o, if he wasn't dead, then he was only wounded.

"What are you doing?" Fiona sounded more puzzled than worried.

"Just get an ambulance," he told her, getting a mouthful of grass at the same time.

"What for?"

Jesus! What for! "I've been shot!"

"Where?"

Where? Where? What did it matter where? What mattered was, he'd been shot. Shot! In the... well, where had he been lot?

"I don't know," Arthur admitted. "Have a look."

Fiona knelt and ran her hands over his body. Arthur rather liked it. Then he remembered that he'd been shot, and began to look for the wound himself. His knee ached bit. But he'd fallen on that. After more searching, while Raymonde and Bernaard hovered anxiously about, he had to admit that he could find no wound. Neither could Fiona.

"I heard a shot," Arthur said defensively.

"I think it was a car backfiring," Fiona told him.

"Ah...." Arthur got up. He felt silly. He brushed bits of grass off his trousers and wondered what to say. Several passers-by had stopped to watch him when he fell. Probably hoping against hope that he'd throw a really spectacular fit.

For their benefit he held up one foot and pointed to his sole. "New shoes," he said loudly. "Ha! Slippery new shoes." Unconvinced, his audience petered away.

Arthur moved on, doggedly. Fiona clung to his arm protectively and lovingly. Arthur wished she wouldn't He wanted to be alert, free, on the balls of his feet, read] to dive for cover at the slightest sign of trouble. Fiona on his arm left him as manoeuvrable as a man with a crutch But she clung so firmly, and smiled at him so bravely, he couldn't tell her.

Raymonde and Bernaard prowled around them like angry bears. They crouched slightly as they walked, and tried to avoid staining their highly polished shoes on the grass. All passers-by were given a steely stare. Anything suspicious was investigated. No one escaped. Nannies had their pram contents inspected. Newspaper readers found their copies thrust aside to reveal their faces. Lovers were turned over with the tip of a brightly polished, slightly grass-soiled shoe, for similar inspection. Even small boys in shorts were given the once-over—though in their case Arthur was slightly suspicious of the brothers' motives.

Black was playing a waiting game. He and Mull shadowed Arthur's group from a parallel path, some fifty yards behind.

Mull was enjoying himself. He liked zoos. He hoped the excursion would go past the elephant enclosures. He liked elephants especially. He wondered if Detective Inspector Black had a favourite animal, but he decided not to ask.

Black wasn't thinking about animals at all. He was thinking about Arthur. The man was a menace. Three deaths—the police sergeant, the caretaker, and the bouncer—had a direct connection with Harris. Everywhere the man went, he le! bodies. And yet here he was, this… character, walking around with two of the biggest crooks in London, looking at blood animals! Black ground his teeth. "I'll kill him," he muttered to himself. "I'll kill him."

Fifty yards behind him, the odd job man was muttering much the same.

Bernaard raised the alarm when they reached the kangaroos.

Marsupials, actually, Arthur reminded himself. Pouched animals. They were housed in a modern glass "cage." Arthur examined them, then read the explanatory notice. One of nature's mistakes, he decided. For a moment he forgot all about the odd job man.

Then Bernaard whirled around with a swish of gravel, his face bulging with desire for speech.

Arthur stared at him. "What?" he demanded.

"I've j… j… j… j…."

Arthur took a deep breath, and tried to be calm. But his voice still emerged as a squeak: "Please stop stuttering!" Bernaard turned to him, his face abject. "I'm sor… sorr…."

Arthur appealed to Raymonde: "Please, what's he on about? My life *is* in danger."

Raymonde gripped his brother by the arms, and peered at him. "What's up?" he demanded.

"I've just s… s… s… s…."

"Seen?" Raymonde guessed.

"Ye… ye…."

"Yes!" Raymonde turned to Arthur, his face alight. "He's just seen something. Or someone. Through the glass of this cage, I suppose."

"What? Who?" Arthur was dancing with impatience.

"Come on, Bernaard!" Raymonde shook his huge brother. "What did you see?"

"M… m… m…."

"A man?" Asked Raymonde.

Bernaard nodded vigorously. "M… m…."

"Two men?"

This time he shook his head. "M… m…."

"Oh, for Christ's sake!" Arthur looked to heaven, then to Fiona, then to the marsupials. Lucky little bastards! He thought. No one's trying to kill them. None of them stutter.

He turned back to Raymonde, furious. "Ask him!" he hissed. "Ask him!"

"Now, look…," Raymonde began to calm Arthur—then froze, staring over his shoulder. Arthur whirled but could see no one. He turned back.

"What…?"

But Raymonde was checking with Bernaard.

"You've just seen Mull?"

"Y… y… y…."

Raymonde turned back to Arthur. And he said something that Arthur found utterly incredible: "The job's off. There's a copper here we know."

"WHAT???"

"The job's off."

And then, after saying something so incredible, he and Bernaard began to do something absolutely impossible. They turned and began to *walk away*.

Arthur scrabbled after them. "You can't leave now!" he pleaded. "You *can't*."

But they did.

Black saw them go, and nudged Mull into action.

"You take the brothers," he ordered. "I'll follow Harris."

"Right." Mull bombed off. Then he bombed rapidly back. "Wait a minute. They've split up."

So they had. "Right," Black ordered. "You follow the one with the stutter, I'll take the other. We'll get Harris later."

They sprinted away down the path, back towards the exit. After thirty yards, Detective Inspector Black found that Sergeant Mull had not followed Bernaard, as instructed. Instead both policemen were following Raymonde.

"What are you doing?" he panted angrily, already out of breath. He pointed after Raymonde. "*He* hasn't got the stutter!"

Mull had had enough of this. Moan moan moan! Bitch bitch bitch! Black couldn't leave him alone. Well, he'd had enough.

He turned so that he was running backwards. That way he could look directly into Black's eyes, as he shouted out his reasonable, logical and watertight defence:

"How am I supposed to tell at this distance?"

Lumbering away heavily into the distance, the Bennet brothers disappeared.

Snapping, griping, stumbling, the two policemen ran, at first together, then separately, and finally they too vanished from view.

Arthur and Fiona stood alone by the marsupials, gazing after the fleeing figures.

Arthur swallowed. They'd gone. Now only three of them were left. Fiona, himself, and the odd job man. Well, the whole thing had begun with the three of them. So with the three of them, let it end.

Seventeen

Arthur felt exposed, vulnerable. He began to be very afraid. He grabbed Fiona's hand, and together they trotted deeper into the zoo. Arthur heard his breath rasping in his throat, and sweat trickled into his eyes. Everywhere seemed to be wide open spaces of concrete, edged with grass. Everything seemed to be flat and broad. For a moment he visualized himself and Fiona as two little models on the top of a wedding cake. As he ran he searched constantly for a glimpse of the odd job man, turning one way then the other, but he couldn't see him. This was cold comfort. He'd be there, somewhere. He always was. They jogged on. Lions, tigers, hippos. Arthur hated them all. A zoo was a terrible place to die.

Fiona tugged at his hand. She was gasping, and at first he couldn't understand what she wanted. Then he saw that she was pulling him towards a building. It looked different to the others. He caught a glimpse of the sign. "Nocturnal Animal House." He didn't know what it meant, and didn't care. Fiona was right, it was a bolt hole. Out in the open he might be shot any moment. Inside, surely he'd be safer.

Still holding hands, they went into the entrance, and down some steps. And found themselves in total darkness.

No... not total. Arthur realized after a few seconds that some faint light was coming from glass cases. Of course—nocturnal animals. No wonder it was dark. As his eyes began to adjust, Arthur could see they were not alone in the building. Vague figures loomed in the darkness. But none were recognizable or definite.

Arthur took a deep breath. This was better. The odd job man would never find him in a place like this.

"Mr. Harris." The odd job man's voice came to him through the darkness like the knell of doom.

Arthur whipped around—and made a terrible mistake. He let go of Fiona's hand.

"Mr. Harris?"

He froze. Where was Fiona? Where did the voice come from? For that matter, where was he? He turned in a slow circle, cautiously extending his arms. He touched no one. But in the murk he could still half-sense, half-see other human figures.

"Mr. Harris!"

This time Arthur got a fix on the voice. He peered, and his heart leaped. A dim little figure, over to his right. Arthur smiled grimly to himself. A *very* dim little figure.

"Mr. Harris!!" It was almost a whisper, tense and penetrating. Arthur clenched his right fist. He paused, now sensing another figure, to his left. That must be Fiona.

He reached across to her, and took her hand. Then, leading her at arm's length, he edged gently forward towards the odd job man.

"Mr. Harris?"

Arthur said loudly: "Just a minute...," and then stepped forward and swung his fist with all his strength. He felt it strike a body, glance off, and hit a face. There was a scream, and somebody fell.

"Come on, Fiona!" he yelled, and ran for the exit, dragging her behind him. Together they pounded up the steps. Someone at the top opened the door, and daylight poured in on them. Arthur turned to smile encouragement at Fiona, and found himself grinning into the face of the odd job man.

One of the odd job man's hands was firmly clasped in his. The other held a revolver. With terrifying deliberation, the odd job man raised the gun until it pointed straight at Arthur's face. He could actually see a short way down the barrel.

Arthur dropped the little man's hand and ran like a stag. He burst out of the building, shot across a patch of grass, and then tore up a path and round a corner. A long straight avenue stretched in front of him, crowded with parties of zoo-goers. Head down, he pounded up the path, dodging around people where necessary, pushing through them, once leaping over a pushchair, and all the time moving just as fast as he could.

He came to another turn-off, and glanced back. A hundred yards down the path the odd job man was involved in an argument with one of the groups that Arthur had pushed through. They were foreigners. Swedes, perhaps. Big blond men, who objected to being pushed about, were jabbing angry fingers at the little man in the leather coat. He was trying to get away, to catch Arthur, but they stood firmly in his way.

Arthur laughed briefly. Then he put his head down again, and ran strongly on across the zoo, aiming for one of the side exits.

He thought guiltily about Fiona. If that had been the odd job man's hand which he'd grabbed in the dark, then the person he'd thumped must have been… oh, dear. And then to rush away, to abandon her like that…. Still, perhaps it was for the best. This way she was out of it. He had drawn the pursuit away from her. She was safe. In rushing away, he had only been thinking of her.

But that wasn't true. Arthur couldn't delude himself. He hadn't been thinking of her. He had been thinking of him. And of staying alive.

He found what he was looking for—a revolving gate of high metal bars, and he slipped through this and out into the street. It was a relief to get out. A zoo, he thought again, was a terrible place to die. But now, looking around, he found he didn't know where he was. This was ridiculous. It was the Regent's Park area, wasn't it? Just a little north from where he lived. And yet this particular street was totally new to him. He cursed. How was it possible that one could live in London for years and never know what was just around the corner? He wondered which way to run.

Then salvation appeared at the end of the street—a taxi, with its "For Hire" light glowing.

Arthur leaped into the road and waved his hands like a wild man. The taxi came to a shuddering halt. Arthur limped up to the driver's window, gasped out his address, and reached thankfully for the door. The driver's hand beat him to it, closing possessively on the handle.

"Only Tottenham," he said.

"What?"

"I'm on me way home. I'll take you if you're going Tottenham way. Nowhere else."

"But... but...," Arthur couldn't believe it. "Please!" he begged. "I'll pay you extra—please!"

"Sorry." The driver had a face which had never registered the emotion of regret in its entire life.

"But you've got your light on!" Arthur said with sudden righteousness. "You've got to take me. Your light's on."

The driver switched the light off. "No, it's not," he said. "Tottenham only." He let out the clutch, and the taxi rumbled away.

Arthur stood in the road, looking after it. He shouted: "And you've got a rotten football team, too!"

but he was far too late, and he doubted if the man heard.

But, as if *he* had heard, the odd job man and his motor-cycle combination turned the corner at the top of the street and roared down on Arthur like a war chariot.

Arthur ran. He ran away down the street' then crossed over and fled up a side street, down an alleyway, diagonally across another street, into a fourth. He was conscious of only two things. One, that he was heading south, towards home, which still somehow represented safety. Two, that he had to keep running and stay in front of the motorcycle, at all costs.

At first luck was with him. He progressed down a series of short streets, each of which met a major road. Arthur was able to sprint across through the traffic. The odd job man had to stop and wait.

A one-way street proved even more useful. Arthur dashed up it the wrong way, but the odd job man came to a halt at the signs, wheeled round, and made a time-wasting detour. Arthur gained fifty yards.

But it couldn't last. Arthur was more tired than he had ever been. He gasped for air, and his legs were like dough. There was a note of triumph in the revs of the motorcycle combination, as it closed up behind him.

With the cold hand of death on his shoulder, Arthur decided to go to ground. He swerved suddenly on the pavement, and crashed through the half-open door of a shop. He skidded to a halt. The place was a garden store. Plants, vases, bags of fertilizer, bamboo canes. He looked around for somewhere to hide. There was a small counter and, sitting behind it, a girl in a blue overall. She was reading a paperback book and didn't look up. She was far too young to be of any practical help. Arthur ignored her, and ran on through the shop, and out the back. The girl didn't look up, even when a motorcycle combination roared to a halt outside, idled for a moment, then revved up and moved on.

Arthur found himself in a garden centre. He'd never seen anything like it. To a flat dweller like him, it was a foreign land. A land ringed with mountain ranges of rockery stones, studded with greenhouse cities, criss-crossed with roads of multi-coloured paving stones, forested by conifers in pots, and peopled by... yes, by gnomes! Hundreds and hundreds of gnomes. Sitting gnomes, squatting gnomes, fishing gnomes, waving gnomes. Gnomes dancing in a ring, gnomes playing leapfrog over each other, gnomes playing leapfrog over a frog, gnomes digging, gnomes wielding scythes, one gnome actually on a bicycle, and dozens and dozens more gnomes just standing there, gnomishly.

The place had one failing. There was no back way out. A huge wall ran right round the garden. Just too high to climb.

Arthur nearly panicked, at the thought that he had run into a trap. Then, against one wall, he spotted a little figure that actually wasn't a gnome. It was a nude girl—a statue, he realized a split second later, and about three-quarters life size. The think stood in an attitude of clumsy allure, displaying two perfect uptilted breasts, but covering its pubic mound with two modestly clasped hands.

Arthur ran at it. He stuck his right food in the clasped hands and heaved upwards, grasping the top of the wall. Then, using the left uptilted boob as another foothold, he levered himself to the top of the wall. The nipple broke off at the last moment, but Arthur straddled the wall, flung his legs and hips across, and lowered himself scrapingly down the other side. His feet touched the ground, and he sagged thankfully against the wall and closed his eyes in momentary relief.

Then he turned and found himself staring into the face of the odd job man. The little man looked equally surprised. He was sitting on his motorbike, at the kerbside. Once again with slow deliberation he raised his gun and pointed it at Arthur. Then he closed his eyes, and his hand tightened around the trigger.

Arthur literally crawled up the wall.

He was back over the top and sliding down the other side before he heard the shot.

He ran and crouched behind a pile of stone, wondering if the odd job man could climb the wall. There was one brief scrabble from the other side, then silence. Then the odd job man's hand appeared over the top, gripping the gun—and fired it!

A gnome squatting on a toadstool disintegrated into slivers of plastic.

Arthur gasped.

Bang! A gnome fishing on a bridge across a pond tipped forward into the water.

Bang! A gnome carrying water from the well suddenly found its head in its bucket.

Arthur ran for more cover. The man had gone mad. He was shooting wild. How long would it be before that stupid girl in the shop called the police? Too long, he thought bitterly. Too long.

He found good cover. Back up towards the building there stood a select little grotto. Here the gnomes weren't gnomes, they were the Seven Dwarfs. In doleful attitude they stood around a little bier on which slept a plastic Snow White. Arthur flattened himself behind the bier. Appropriate! Slightly hysterically he laughed out loud. The dwarfs looked back on him, in their characteristic attitudes.

There was silence from the other side of the wall. Arthur raised his head slightly. The hand and the gun still poked over the top. Arthur called: "Odd job man! Can you hear me?"

Bang! A cascade of plastic. Happy died laughing.

Arthur realized that by shouting, he had given the odd job man a rough aiming point. But he had to go on.

"I want you to stop doing this!"

Bang! Doc became suddenly incurable.

"Listen, please!"

Bang! Dopey never knew what hit him.

"I've changed my mind!"

Bang! Sneezy caught a cold.

"I don't want to die anymore!"

Silence.

Encouraged, Arthur continued: "I want you to forget that I told you to ignore everything I said. Ignore it. I don't mean it any longer. I don't want to die. I want to live."

He paused again. Still silence. At last! he thought thankfully. I'm getting through to him. I've convinced him. I'm safe.

Bang! Grumpy stopped grumbling.

Arthur realized that the odd job man had not been listening. He'd been re-loading. He tried again.

"Please stop it!"

Bang! Bashful bowed out of the limelight.

"You've got to...."

Bang! Sleepy went for the big sleep.

"Please!"

Bang! Snow White got hers. It would, Arthur thought madly, take more than a kiss to restore her to life. It would take a tube of Evostick.

He got to his feet. The plastic bier was no protection. He looked around for somewhere more solid.

But then he realized that the gun and the hand had disappeared. The odd job man had ceased firing. Then with a roar the combination burst into life. Was he leaving…? No. The engine rumbled for a moment, then stopped again. Arthur wondered what the odd job man was playing at. Then he saw. Two hands appeared at the top of the wall. Then the beret.

Turning, running, Arthur realized that the odd job man had driven his combination up onto the pavement, and was standing on it to help him climb over the wall.

The chase was on again.

But this time, Arthur thought as he raced back through the shop and on down the road, at least he had a good start. Before the odd job man could get back to his bike, he'd be a quarter of a mile away. Head down, jogging steadily, he set out for home.

Five minutes later, out of breath but happier, he was jogging across the flats forecourt. He paused on the entrance step and looked around, satisfied that he had shaken off pursuit.

With a roar the combination swept into the forecourt.

"Aaaah!" Despite himself, Arthur cried out. Then he turned and ran for the lift. He jabbed at the button, but the thing wouldn't come. He sensed the shadow of the odd job man entering the hall. The stairs! He sprinted away up them. First one flight, then another. And another.

Now exhaustion had him by the throat. On the third landing he staggered, then pushed the lift button.

Almost immediately, and blessedly, the bell pinged.

The doors opened. Gun waving, the odd job man sprang out. Gasping, Arthur staggered in.

Both turned and gaped at each other. The lift doors closed.

Sobbing, Arthur pushed the button for his floor. The lift started up again.

If only he could stay in the lift, he thought desperately. But of course the doors always opened. Bloody automatic doors! He cursed the whole concept of automation. Then, grimly, he braced himself against the back wall of the lift. He put a foot up against it for extra propulsion, and waited.

The lift stopped. The doors opened.

Arthur shot out, and collided bodily with the odd job man.

The little man fell like a skittle, and Arthur plunged on top of him. The gun! That was the important thing. That was the only thing. He got a hand round the odd job man's wrist, then two hands. The odd job man brought his other hand up, to tear at Arthur's. They rolled around on the landing, struggling for the gun, their voices rasping in each other's ears.

"I've changed...," Arthur began, but then a flying knee caught him in the groin, and he yelped.

"Don't fi...." The odd job man tried, but Arthur got an elbow into the man's mouth, and ground down on it with all the strength he had.

But the odd job man still had the gun. Arthur knew that unless he could somehow get his own hands on it, the little man would win in the end. Desperately he tightened his grip. The rolling over and over slowly stopped, and, with the disputed weapon trembling between them, they rose first to their knees, then to their feet.

The tension in Arthur's arms made his muscles ache and his body shake. He looked into the odd job man's eyes. They flashed back at him. Arthur thought of all the fear and the misery and the apprehension that these eyes had caused him during the past days, and he was gripped with a raging animal fury.

He raised the odd job man's gun-gripping hands high over his head, until the man's toes must have been leaving the floor. Then he shouted at him, and as he shouted, he jerked the hands backwards and forwards to the rhythm of his words.

"Listen—you—sod—I—have—changed—my—"

At "my" the gun came loose. The jerk sent it spinning high across the landing, to clatter on the floor by the lift doors.

For a fraction of time Arthur and the odd job man ;ripped hands and stared at it. Then Arthur let the little nan go, and started towards it.

He ran straight into the man's raised knee. It sank deep into his stomach, and drove everything but fear from his body. He sank gasping to his knees, and watched in horror is the little man scampered across the landing, grabbed the gun, turned, and aimed it at his face.

The lift doors opened, Fiona leaped through them like a tigress, and fell on the odd job man.

He collapsed beneath her, squeaking with surprise. Unbelieving, but suddenly renewed and refreshed, Arthur galloped over to join in, and together he and Fiona sat on the odd job man, and pressed the resistance out of him. Arthur didn't speak until he had both the odd job man's arms twisted up behind his back, and a knee on the man's leek. Fiona sat on his rear, and pinned his legs. At last it felt safe to try and explain.

"I've changed my mind," Arthur said.

"He does not want you to kill him," added Fiona.

"Eh?" It seemed a difficult concept for the odd job man to grasp.

"I want to *live*!" Arthur was adamant.

"Oh." Arthur felt the odd job man's muscles suddenly relax beneath him. "*Now* you tell me!"

Fiona climbed carefully off the man, and picked up the gun where it had fallen. She levelled it at the odd job man. Then Arthur got off him, and they both got to their feet.

The odd job man looked nervously at Fiona. "Careful," he warned her. "It's loaded. I want to live as well."

"We all do." There was the slightest tremor in Fiona's voice.

The odd job man knocked some dust from his trousers. "Well," he said brightly, "I'll be off then."

Arthur took a deep breath. "Good…," he began. Then changed it to "Good luck in… the future, then."

"And you." The odd job man's eyes flashed. "And if you ever need any odd jobs, I'll…" Then he thought better of it. "Perhaps not."

Solemnly he shook hands, and they saw him into the lift. When the doors closed, they put their arms around each other, and hugged their relief and their joy.

Then they went back into the flat. Arthur made straight for the drinks cabinet. He up-turned two glasses, found the scotch, took a long delicious swig from the bottle, then poured out two generous measures.

Fiona sank back into an armchair, then reached up for her drink—and discovered that she still held the odd job man's revolver.

"His gun!" Her eyes were wide. "He's forgotten it!"

"Oh, God!" Arthur could suddenly see endless difficulties and complications arising from the wretched gun. He grabbed it from Fiona, and ran out into the corridor. The indicator showed that the lift had reached the ground floor.

He ran back into the flat. "He's gone!"

"Quick! The balcony!" Fiona struggled with the door' catch. "We'll catch him coming out of the building."

Together they ran out onto the balcony and leaned over the rail to peer down. They were just in time to see the ode job man as he walked out into the sunlight.

Arthur waved the gun in the air and yelled at him: "Oi You've forgotten your gun!"

The words echoed around the building, and Arthur clamped his hand to his mouth in embarrassment. Then more quietly, and keeping the gun out of sight, he called again.

"You've left something behind."

The odd job man backed away slightly, his pale face looking up at them.

"What?" they heard him should faintly.

"I said you've left something behind."

The odd job man heard all right this time, but for some reason he didn't seem pleased. He was waving at them agitatedly, almost desperately. He was shouting something, his face screwed up with effort, and now he ran forward until he was directly beneath them. His voice rose to an agonized pitch.

Arthur and Fiona leaned forward to hear what was so dreadfully important.

The section of the balcony rail, which the odd job

man had carefully sawn through, gave way, and tipped them both gently forward into space.

The odd job man saw Arthur and Fiona plunging down to him, and he raised his hands in a futile gesture to ward them off.

Inspector Black, who was being driven into the forecourt by Sergeant Mull, saw them fall. He saw their arms stretched out. He saw the odd job man standing beneath them, his arms raised. And for one instant it seemed to him that they were all reaching out to one another, to help, to comfort, and to hold.

www.ingramcontent.com/pod-product-compliance
Lightning Source LLC
Chambersburg PA
CBHW030818210726
48290CB00002B/645

* 9 7 8 1 9 5 9 2 0 5 4 8 7 *